The Soldier's Seed

Book One
of
Southern Skyes

By
SHARYN BRADFORD LUNN

***The Soldier's Seed**, Southern Skyes Book One*

http://SharynBradfordLunnAuthor.com

Third edition eBook 2012
First edition paperback 2012
Published and printed in the USA by *thewordverve inc.*

Paperback ISBN: 978-0-9857157-7-9
eBook ISBN: 978-0-9872132-4-2

LOC # 2012951165

A Soldier's Seed
A Book with Verve by *thewordverve inc.*

www.thewordverve.com

Cover, artwork, and creative design by
Robin Krauss, Linden Design
www.lindendesign.biz

Foreword

The Soldier's Seed is a work of fiction woven around actual historical events. Nicholas Thomas and his descendants are fictional and any similarity to any person, living or dead, is purely coincidental.

To achieve a degree of historical accuracy, the names of some real people have been included in the narrative. The main ones include:

- Lieutenant Governor Philip Gidley King
- Lieutenant Governor John Bowen
- Lieutenant Governor David Collins
- Miss Martha Hayes
- Lieutenant William Moore

Creative licence has been used in relation to statements and conversations attributed to these persons, but their essence is largely factual.

The Pallitteeler band is entirely fictional, but every effort has been made to portray the customs and beliefs of the First Tasmanians as accurately as possible.

The Southern Skyes series is dedicated to the First Tasmanians

AUSTRALIA
Sydney Town
Bass Straight
Furne aux
Islands
King's Island
Port
Dalrymple
Launceston
Norfolk Plains
Van Diemen's
Land
New
Norfolk
Risdon
Hobart
Bruny Island

THE DERWENT ESTUARY

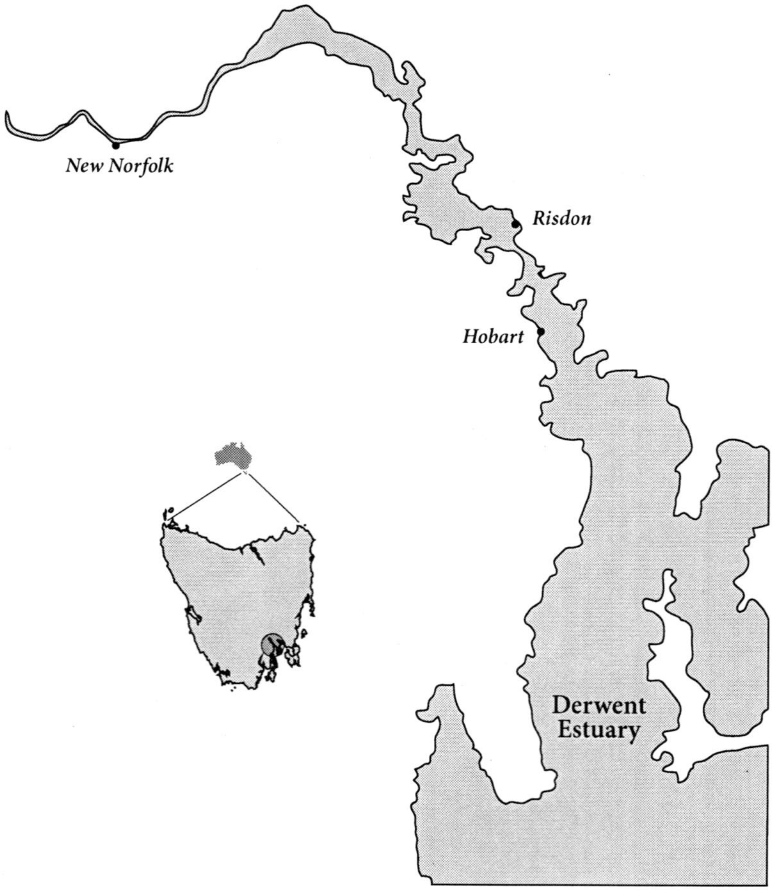

VAN DIEMEN'S LAND

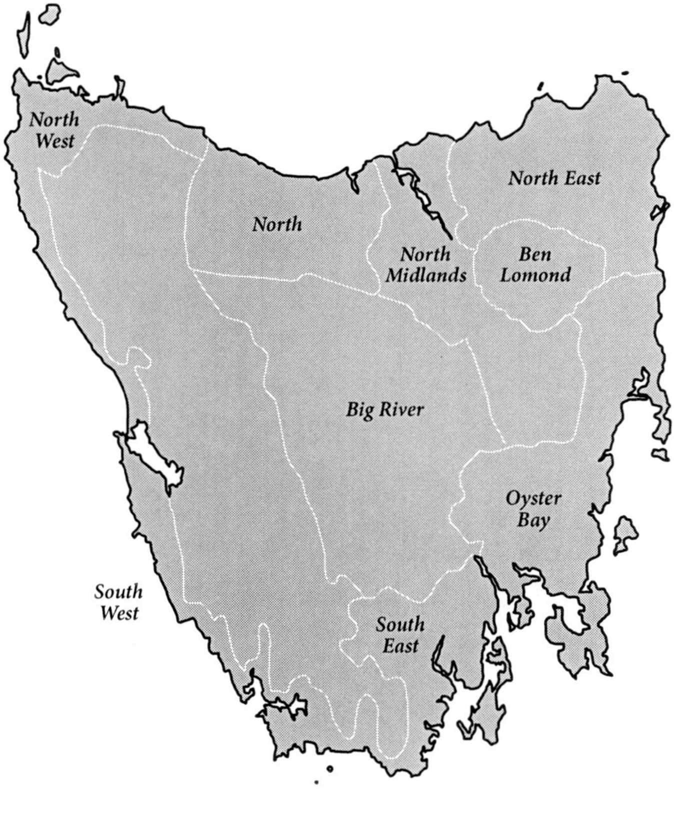

Aboriginal Tribal Boundries

Chapter 1

Sydney Town 1803

Raucous laughter wrenched Nicholas Thomas from the depths of unconsciousness, and with a reflex action, he swung his legs from the wooden bunk where he had collapsed in a drunken stupor only hours before. He knew he shouldn't drink—had told himself this countless times—even promised that he would never drink again, but at his core he knew he would drink again. He couldn't NOT drink again.

Without opening his eyes, he groped the dusty floorboards for the red jacket with yellow trim that indicated his status of private in the New South Wales Corps. A blast of pain speared through his head. He grimaced, hung his head, and stared down between his knees, but there was little regret for last night's carousing.

The clamour outside continued, and conscious of the late hour, Nicholas ran a pair of callused hands through his thick, yellow curls and rose cautiously to his feet. A heady throbbing encompassed him, and he swayed, steadied himself on the roughly hewn post in the centre of the hut and cursed his raging thirst.

It was not his first encounter with the aftermath of inebriation. Since his arrival in New South Wales, it had become a frequent occurrence, and even for a one-time teetotaller from a Kentish farm, this was not considered unusual. The corps always changed a man—mostly for the worse. In Nicholas' case, a morning of misery following a night of rum held less pain than his abysmal existence in Sydney Town. Any measure of contentment he once knew vanished the moment he set foot on these accursed shores. Memories of happier times in another life belonged to another world left thousands of miles away. Whether he drank to forget the memories or his current situation, he could no longer tell—not that it really mattered.

The throbbing diminished, and Nicholas again became aware of the racket outside. Laughter and mocking voices, coupled with the incessant barking of dogs, filled his ears as he slipped an arm into the colourful jacket and yanked it over his dusty, white shirt. Despite his rough stubble, he decided shaving could wait. He thrust aside the canvas-backed door and stepped out toward the commotion.

The fist that collided with his jaw and sent him reeling back into the hut came from somewhere within the blinding sunlight that greeted him. "You bastard," an enraged voice bellowed as Nicholas crashed backward, only managing to stay upright because his back slammed against the centre post. "This is the first and only warning you'll get. Keep away from my wife or your days are numbered. Do I make myself clear?"

Nicholas recognised his red-faced assailant as Stuart Thornridge, a storekeeper on George Street. He struggled to regain his senses, but slipped down the post, the strength draining from his legs. "You've got it all wrong," he slurred. "I haven't seen her in ages." It was a poor attempt at a bluff, but he had nothing better to offer. "What makes you think there's something going on anyway?" he asked, attempting to scramble out of reach, but only managed to stumble off to the side of the post before Thornridge lunged at him.

"Don't try to lie to me, boy," he bellowed, shoving Nicholas backward.

Nicholas' arms flailed in a vain attempt to stay upright, but his heels caught the side of a small storage chest by his bunk and sent him sprawling again. This time he made no attempt to regain his feet as the man's onslaught continued.

"My wife told me everything."

"What? Emmeline wou—" Nicholas blurted, feeling the bottom fall out of his stomach. Still on his backside, he floundered awkwardly toward the rear of the hut.

"Her conscience got the better of her," Thornridge snarled. "And it's Mrs. Thornridge to you. If it wasn't for her pleading, I'd beat you to a pulp right now, so if I ever hear you've been anywhere near her again, that's exactly what I'll do. Furthermore," he paused, sweeping Nicholas with a look of total contempt, "if the child she's carrying arrives with your wiry, yellow frizz, you're a dead man."

Nicholas felt his throat close and his chest constrict. He gasped and tried to make some sense of what he heard. Emmeline carrying his child? But before he could think it through, his attention was hauled back to the figure towering over him. Given Thornridge's size, Nicholas had no doubt the man could make good his threat and found himself once more backing away, this time with bile scorching the back of his throat. "There's no truth in it," he stammered, hating himself for lying and even more for cowering in the face of the man's fury.

Thornridge stared at his victim's crab-like retreat. "What she ever saw in such a pathetic excuse for a man, let alone a soldier, is beyond me," he snarled, scorn distorting his face. "And I'll not waste more time on the likes of a drunken coward. You've had fair warning." With that, he abruptly turned and left the hut.

Nicholas gingerly felt his jaw as the door banged closed. The man had one hell of a punch. His thoughts returned to Emmeline. He had been swept off his feet by her dark, sensual, beauty, had adored everything about her, and had eagerly jumped into her bed, but Emmeline had never been entirely honest with him, neglecting to mention her betrothal to the older, more prosperous, Stuart Thornridge. When the truth came out, a devastated Nicholas turned again to alcohol, vowing never to see her again. Of course he had seen the new Mrs. Thornridge from afar, and even though his heart decreed otherwise, he avoided contact.

But what if Emmeline was carrying his child? If he really was the father, she would have to be well on the way now, so no wonder Thornridge questioned the child's paternity. Again Nicholas swallowed bile.

The noise down the road pulled his attention back to the present. There was no time to dwell on Emmeline now. God knows he had already done enough of that. Quickly he strode to the door, this time checking for Thornridge's absence before proceeding.

Chapter 2

Shafts of sunlight streamed through the few remaining trees on the point where the corps was based. The smell of dust hung in the hot, dry air. Nicholas squinted through bloodshot eyes toward the harbour of Port Jackson, its deep, blue-green waters shimmering in the heat. Three tall ships, their sails furled, lay anchored and idle. In front of him, at the bottom of the slope, the Tank Stream trickled fresh water into the sea while surrounded by the growing harbour town of Sydney. A short distance down the well-worn track leading to the waterfront was the source of the noise.

Several men from the Royal Marines gathered with a group of the corps beneath the trees adjacent to the mess hut. It was not often the corps had casual visitors from the marines, so such an event had to herald significant news. Nicholas hurried toward them, still struggling to get his left arm into his jacket. Despite the laughter the atmosphere was tense. Rivalry between the two services had existed since the corps' inception fourteen years ago when Major Grose was commissioned to establish a new military unit in New South Wales to replace the uncooperative marines who had arrived with the first fleet only a year before.

The marines considered themselves too good to supervise convicts and looked down on the New South Wales Corps, which was formed to do precisely that, and the corps resented the snooty, condescending attitude of the marines. As a result, they barely tolerated each other and rarely socialized. Nicholas could only assume they were here to crow about something, and it was probably to do with recent rumours.

The gossip of recent weeks was that Governor King was about to dispatch a newly arrived lieutenant, by the name of John Bowen, to Van Diemen's Land to establish a settlement on the Derwent River and forestall French colonisation of the area. Rumour had it that the military force to accompany Bowen would be drawn from the New South Wales Corps.

"Well, it's definite," the redheaded marine jeered. "The Derwent has to be settled so we can keep those damned Frogs out, and you stupid bastards are the ones who get to go down there." Another howl of laughter came from the marine's six mates.

"You'll get the worst of the convicts," another hooted, slapping his thigh. "Anyone of use will be kept 'ere. You'll be in charge of nothing but degenerates and no-hopers," he spluttered as the others reeled about. Nicholas scowled. He saw through the exaggerated mirth used to provoke a response, as did most of the corps, and knew someone would have to bite.

Ben Rogers got to his feet. Simon Henderson quickly interjected. "It mightn't be so bad," he said from his seated position, motioning Rogers to rejoin him. "I could do wif a bit of adventure . . . blaze a new trail or some'n."

"What the bloody hell do you think we been doin' in New South Wales?" growled a voice from the back of the corps.

"All I'm sayin' is, it's some'n different, to start up a settlement and build a town out of nuthin. Reckon it wouldn't be borin'," Henderson defended. "After all, none of us were 'ere back in 1788 when it all started."

"Thank the Lord," someone grunted.

"I'll drink to that," another followed.

Henderson continued. "There were some marines who transferred over to the corps, who would know what it was really like in the beginnin', but they'd have left the service ages ago. Some settled 'ere on their land grants so with a bit of luck we could track one or two down and 'ave a chat."

"Who gives a damn," growled a man named Knott, chewing on a twig. "But if you have to know, ask Rogers here. He's been around long enough."

"Henderson's right." Jim Hall rose and moved to the centre of the group beside Ben Rogers. "Everyone's learned a hell of a lot during the fifteen years of Sydney Town's existence . . . establishing a colony in Van Diemen's Land shouldn't be as hard as this one was. The same mistakes won't be made twice, mark my words."

"Your words don't count for much," Rogers cut in, glaring at Hall. "Anyway, Bowen's a naval officer . . . fresh off the boat, I hear. He can't be expected to know the ropes yet, and besides, it's sheer lunacy to put him in charge of any part of the New South Wales Corps. We ain't navy. What's the blasted governor thinking? Everyone knows who really runs this place and that includes him, too. No snotty-nosed bastard from the Navy is gonna fare any better against the corps."

Another roar of laughter filled the air, this time from the corps, while the marines regrouped and moved threateningly closer to Rogers.

"The shysters in command of the New South Wales Corps have become too powerful. It's no good for the corps or anyone else here," a marine sneered. "That's no doubt why King's decided to ship some of you out."

It was true the corps was powerful. After the first governor, Arthur Phillip, left New South Wales at the end of his four-year stint, the corps' commanding officer, Francis Grose, became acting governor of the settlement for two years. It was during this time the corps' operations were allowed to expand beyond its original brief of convict discipline and other civilian tasks associated with building the new colony. Grose allocated large land grants to his officers and encouraged them to use convict labour to work the land outside the government farms' normal working hours and pay them in rum. He also supported his officers in private trading, and as a result, they became wealthy landowners and stockholders with a monopoly on the rum trade. While convict discipline always remained the corps' prime brief, large-scale farming and trading, particularly in spirits, produced many wealthy men with avenues for other questionable enterprises, social climbing, and political desires.

Nicholas took a seat with a few other men on a log that served as a fence separating the rough road from the crude garden surrounding the mess hut that had become the corps' unofficial headquarters.

"That sounds like sour grapes to me," scoffed Rogers. "The existence of the corps owes itself to the fact you toffy-nosed marines refused to get your hands dirty. If you'd done your job in the first place, there'd never have been any need for us, now would there?"

"The Royal Marines were never intended for such a role," the redheaded marine stated, placing great emphasis on *royal.*

"Everyone knew that except Governor Phillip, who expected the Marines to be his all-purpose labour force. Our commanding officer had to draw the line somewhere." The redheaded marine tilted his chin skyward. "We are soldiers, not general-purpose lackeys, and Major Ross had to make sure our commission was not abused. We're not going to be keepers of criminals . . . the Royal Marines has a reputation to uphold."

"So why do you suppose you got sent out with the first load of convicts then?" Rogers taunted, watching the young marine's face turn red. Not getting a response, he continued. "The way I see it, the task of maintaining law and order in this convict settlement was first assigned to the Royal Marines, and they failed dismally." He emphasized the word *royal* even more than the redhead, then added, "You're nothing but a bunch of prissy little pansies."

The redhead lunged at the sneering Rogers, who, pleased with his taunts, stood feet astride and hands on his hips. Two other marines scrambled to restrain their colleague, but not before he planted his fist squarely on Rogers' jaw and sent two other corps members reeling. In the ensuing scuffle, Nicholas was knocked from the log, and by the time he regained his feet, the brief foray was over, both parties glaring at each other, fists clenched and emotions high.

While the burly Rogers and the other participants rubbed their bruises, Nicholas, with no strong feelings of loyalty to the corps, surveyed the rough assembly clad in worn, dusty uniforms with little more than apathy. Sure, he was a private in the New South Wales Corps, but there was no sense of pride within him, not even in the darkest recesses of his consciousness. He loathed the corps, Sydney Town, and the vastness of New South Wales. His fondest desire was to finish his term in what he called "this devil's den" as soon as possible and with the least amount of trauma, then return to England and a quiet farming life. Nicholas watched the marines slowly regroup, turn, and head down the slope toward the township amid passionate jeers and contemptuous quips from the corps.

"If we're a thorn in yer side," Rogers shouted after the Royal Marines, "it's of yer own doing."

"You'll get your just desserts in Van Diemen's Land," the antagonistic redhead yelled over his shoulder. "There'll be no free rides for you down there, and all your lurks and perks will be put to an end. Governor King will see to that."

Chapter 3

After the marines disappeared, the men from the corps reassembled to discuss the ramifications of the news. Curious, Nicholas moved in closer. He was fully aware of the importance of the island to the south. Initially it was thought to be part of the mainland, but after Bass and Flinders proved it to be an island, French interest had been sparked. Napoleon Bonaparte sent two vessels on a scientific voyage to explore its east coast, with the apparent intention of colonisation. The English government resented French activity in the area and knew the island must be settled and claimed for England, but had done little about it.

"I reckon the real reason King is sending a party to Van Diemen's Land is to relieve the strain here in New South Wales," Brady volunteered. "There's been between six and seven thousand convicts transported here so far and we've still no proper prisons or places to send second offenders, except for Norfolk Island, which is only big enough for around one thousand people. Van Diemen's Land sounds like the perfect solution. It's bigger, closer, and by all reports, has excellent horticultural and pastoral land. I reckon this French colonisation scare is only givin' the British Government a bit of a hurry up."

Most of the group agreed, including Nicholas. Talk of the need for another penal settlement had been around long before the French demonstrated any genuine intention of establishing a settlement that posed a threat to British sovereignty in the area. Anxiety, where hardened criminals and second offenders were concerned, had increased after the transportation of the worst Irish convicts to Norfolk Island in 1800 and their subsequent failed conspiracy to massacre the officers and seize the island. If anyone had any insight into the situation on Norfolk Island, it was Governor King, who'd spent close to eight years in charge of the settlement; therefore, so his move to establish a more secure location for such convicts could easily be interpreted as simply advancing the obvious destiny of the colony at a rate faster than would have occurred without the aid of the French.

Van Diemen's Land's remoteness and insular nature equipped it well for a rigid penal colony, where the most violent and disruptive prisoners could be exiled with confidence. With its ports closed to commerce, it would afford little means of escape, and prisoners could be well contained and disciplined, leaving no scope for the evil pursuits of both felon and guard as befell New South Wales. Even so, Nicholas had no particular desire to be part of the new venture. It seemed far less complicated to simply finish his three-year term with the corps in Sydney then get the hell out at the first available opportunity. Ships returned to London much more frequently now than they did in past years so. If he kept his nose clean, obtaining a berth on one of them shouldn't pose too great a problem.

Being one of the younger sons in a family of five boys and

three girls, Nicholas had chosen to seek his fortune in one of the Services. It seemed a logical and sensible decision since he possessed no trade and was unlikely to inherit the small family farm upon the death of their father, that privilege being reserved for his older brother John, the firstborn son of Lucas and Harriet Thomas. His parents had sought to have all their boys taught to read and write, so they all attended the nearby church school in preparation for whatever path they chose. Nicholas, attracted to a life in the navy, bade his parents farewell much earlier than expected and headed off for London. On arrival, as luck would have it, he was captured by tales of wealth and adventure in the antipodes and promptly enlisted in a new army called the New South Wales Corps instead. Life in New South Wales was far from the grand escapade he had anticipated. Sydney Town turned out to be a cesspool of villains and prostitutes, where after dark it was virtually impossible to tell criminal from guard. By day the sun was blistering and the flies too sticky to be rid of with one wave of the hand. Not only was the work arduous and distasteful, he had certainly never seen any of the great wealth allegedly available to the corps. In that area, the officers had total monopoly. True, if he chose to remain in the colony when his term expired he would be granted an allotment of land by the governor, but that to him was an eternity away. Besides, he wanted to return to England. In the meantime, he saw little alternative to trying to make the most of his sorry situation.

Then he thought of Thornridge and felt his stomach knot.

The last thing he wanted was to be shipped off to the wilds of Van Diemen's Land, and yet the possibility offered a way out of the situation in which he now found himself. Perhaps it could even be his salvation.

"Do you suppose they'll take the whole regiment?" asked a corps man named Boyd.

"Hardly," proclaimed Rogers. "We're needed right 'ere."

"Yeah, but Bowen's going to need a decent-sized military."

"Be that as it may, I say the corps is far too valuable 'ere," Rogers stated. "King can't afford to split it in half. If he does there'll be total chaos in New South Wales, and he knows it. I doubt a few more 'n twenty of us will get sent."

Boyd scuffed his boots in the dirt, roughly drawing a map of the island in relation to Sydney Town. "How could twenty men establish a town and keep a bunch of convicts in check when they're so isolated?"

"That's Bowen's problem," Rogers shrugged, as the group shuffled closer to peer at the ground.

"Ne'er a truer word was said," laughed Henderson. "I 'ear the lieutenant's still wet behind the ears, not even twenty-three years old. Lord knows 'ow 'e landed such a commission."

"Maybe there's no one else available, and King's in so much of a hurry to beat the French," someone from the back put in.

"Nah, he's either got money or else he's a friend of the governor," retorted Rogers.

"Maybe he's got what it takes," shot in Nicholas, surprising himself. He wasn't usually so forthright, but irritated by his throbbing head and the negativity of the regiment's resident thug, he couldn't hold back. "You're such a bloody cynic. How about giving the man a fair go before you start in on him? Why do you always have to put everyone down?"

"It goes with the territory, Pretty Boy," Ben Rogers snarled. "And I don't see you still bein' the smart-assed optimist you were when you stepped off the boat. Just because the lieutenant is only a year or two older than you, there's no need to give 'im more than his due."

Nicholas had never taken to Benjamin Rogers. The man was a belligerent, loudmouthed bully, always boasting about his achievements and how he had been one of the original corps members recruited by Major Grose. Since then he had reenlisted several times and as a result received a double land grant in the Field-of-Mars area to the northwest of the township. At the governor's discretion, he had also been assigned the privilege of receiving a year's supply of free clothing, provisions, seed, and grain, as well as three assigned convict servants to maintain the property. With such assistance, Rogers was able to run the farm as well as engage in trading. Several times he had been in a group partnership that had bought the entire cargo from a trading ship and later sold it in Sydney Town at enormous profit.

Rum was the most popular cargo because of its inflated market value, and it appeared to Nicholas that Rogers and most of the New South Wales Corps intended to keep a monopoly on it. The double-dealing and deception that accompanied the total control of alcohol disgusted him, but not as much as Rogers' favourite tale about the Hawkesbury River aboriginal wars, which was the real cause of Nicholas' abhorrence toward him.

When the infant white settlement expanded further inland during the early 1790s in search of more pasture land, aboriginal resentment had escalated and anxious settlers retaliated. Confrontations were frequent, particularly against the Durak tribe of the Hawkesbury River area to the north of Sydney Town, who were said to be particularly aggressive. When open warfare broke out, Rogers, along with approximately one quarter of the corps, were sent to the area under the command of Captain William Paterson. Their orders were to destroy as many of the Durak as possible—and this they did to the best of their ability. Rogers delighted in recounting how he had slain several children by smashing their skulls with the butt of his rifle after shooting the unarmed adults who ran out of spears while defending themselves. Had he been able to wipe out the total aboriginal population single-handed, Nicholas was certain Rogers would have done so, such was his hatred for them.

"This man, Bowen, deserves a fair chance, that's all I'm saying," Nicholas persisted, firm in his gaze at the malevolent face of Rogers. "You've written him off already just because he's young—and a naval officer. You're forgetting he's just returned from a stint on Norfolk Island as acting governor, so he must have some ability."

Few of the corps held much respect for John Bowen. Besides being a navy man, he was considered far too young to have attained the rank of lieutenant, let alone governor. Having entered the navy at the age of fourteen, he arrived in Sydney Town last March with less than ten years' experience under his belt and was quickly dispatched to Norfolk Island to relieve its commanding officer, Lieutenant Joseph Foveaux. To most people's minds, he was ill-equipped for the rank of lieutenant and could hardly possess the skills necessary for the responsible establishment of a new penal colony in the wilds of Van Diemen's Land. Only the governor, it seemed, had any confidence in the young man's ability.

"Time will tell us exactly what the Honourable Lieutenant John Bowen is made of," Rogers sneered. "And if you hold such kinship for the navy, perhaps you should 'ave signed on with them instead of the corps, Private Thomas. Since your arrival, you've done nothing but whine, and the truth of it is, we've had a gut-full of you and your bloody moaning. Wallowin' in self-pity 'll only get you an early grave in this godforsaken place, so you're best to pull yourself together and make the best of whatever the corps and this colony has to offer and stop pretendin' to be such a bloody, self-righteous little prig. Everyone knows about you and Emmeline Thornridge, so stop trying to be Mister Goody Two Shoes."

Rogers' accurate stab at the truth, right down to his being better suited to the navy, hit Nicholas nearly as hard as Thornridge's blow. His head spun with the realization he had been exposed to the entire group. Embarrassed and dumbfounded, he clenched his teeth against Rogers' words and every other raw wound inflicted by the colony and its malicious ways. His gut writhed, but he was not going to crumble under Rogers' bullying tactics. Not this time.

Nicholas quietly rose from the log and, holding his head high, glared at his smirking adversary and the silent onlookers. Some of them thought he was about to plant his fist in Rogers' beard, but instead Nicholas turned toward the mess hut.

As he strode past the group, he failed to notice someone's boot swing out until he had already stumbled and the ground rushed to greet him. Within seconds a jostling crowd converged on him, and hands grabbed the back of his jacket in an attempt to haul him to his feet. Nicholas swung his fists wildly, making little impact as his body was pummelled, and a kick in the backside sent him to the ground again. He was about to curl into a protective ball when his attackers suddenly stepped aside to reveal Rogers.

"Looks like it's time to grow up, Sonny Boy," he scoffed.

"Yeah, man up and stop being the ladies' man, Pretty Boy," someone else said.

A hoot of laughter went up as Nicholas scrambled past their knees toward the mess and followed him inside after the canvas sheet that served as a door flapped down behind him. Despite his efforts to block them out, their jeers continued as he staggered forward and leaned against a table, utterly humiliated.

"It serves 'im right."

"No one's going to baby 'im anymore."

"... can't go 'round moanin' forever ..."

"... do 'im good to get sent south with Bowen."

"Rumour has it that he's got Old Man Thornridge's new wife up the duff . . . reckon he'll be growin' up real quick when that giant comes after him."

Another roar of laughter went up.

"His head won't be stayin' on his shoulders much longer, that's for sure."

Chapter 4

Nicholas regained his composure, but anger still burned deep inside. He poured a mug of tea from the boiling brew on the wood-burner stove. No sooner had he sat down at one of the long mess tables when James Hall swung the canvas aside and entered the room.

"You all right?" he enquired, stepping into the hut. "Don't take it too hard, Nick. They're as frustrated as we are and needed to take it out on someone. Bad luck today it's you. It'll be some other poor bastard tomorrow. Best to just forget it."

"You sticking up for them?"

"You know better 'n to ask that."

Jim Hall was the only friend Nicholas had made since arriving in New South Wales, and then probably only because they were mostly being assigned the same tasks. It was not that Nicholas was normally disagreeable, just that the colony seemed to bring out the worst in him. Jim, who twelve months earlier recognised his new colleague's despair as something similar to what he himself had endured, had taken the young rookie under his wing.

Of course, not everyone plunged to the depths of depression and misery upon disembarking. Most took to Sydney Town and its skulduggery as smoothly as a canoe to deep water, especially after dark when rum, gambling, and strumpets abounded, but a few, like Nicholas and previously Jim, found the place abhorrent and adjustment a continual battle. For these men, sobriety became decidedly unwelcome during their off-duty hours, despite the values they may have once held.

"They're probably right anyway," Nicholas lamented, staring down at the now lukewarm fluid in the tin mug on the bench before him, again aware of his splitting head. "I've brought it all on myself. They can't stand me; I can't even stand myself. I've even joined the ranks of the full-time drunkards just to dodge the realities of this wretched place for a while, but even that doesn't help because in the end I'm so disgusted with myself, the place seems twice as bad, if that's possible. And to make it worse, Emmeline is probably carrying my child. Thornridge paid me a visit this morning, made his feelings quite clear. Just as well my family's not here to witness this." Nicholas continued to stare into the remnants of his tea while Jim remained silent. Minutes passed, then with a sudden change of heart he continued, "Seeing as I'm so unpopular here, perhaps it's not such a bad idea for me to ship out to Van Diemen's Land after all. I might as well volunteer for it; at least that way I can start afresh, well away from the Thornridges."

"There's no need to go to that extreme. All you've got to do is make an effort to join in with whatever's going on. The blokes aren't that bad, you know," Jim encouraged. "If I can get used to it, so can you."

"Maybe I don't want to. Besides, you're forgetting Stuart

Thornridge. Emmeline's pregnant, and he's threatened to kill me if the kid looks like me."

"I doubt he'd stoop to murder—and duelling is not exactly legal."

Nicholas grunted. As far as he was concerned, his future in Sydney Town was now too bleak to contemplate. Even without the Emmeline problem, how he could ever get ahead and make a decent living without resorting to the wheeler-dealings for which the corps had become so notorious, he didn't know. The corps held the seat of power right up the ranks to the governor, and even his power could be curtailed if it suited the officers. The New South Wales Corps, now known as the Rum Corps, had created difficulties from the start, and by 1795, the abuse of power concerned the British government to the extent that it commissioned John Hunter as the second governor of New South Wales, ordering him to restore discipline. He failed to do so, and in 1800, Philip Gidley King attempted to do better. Few inroads were made. If the government could be repeatedly thwarted by the corps, Nicholas could see no way he could win. It was either join them or be crushed, both financially and in spirit, under the relentless onslaught of the greedy power mongers.

"I'm just a simple farm boy," Nicholas said. "It's not for me, all this cheating, wheeling and dealing." He looked Jim squarely in the eye. "You know how they take advantage of both convicts and settlers in the name of the corps. So there isn't much in the way of material gain left for privates like us. The officers have it sewn up with their swindling would-be-honest people out of what little they have just to line their own pockets. And they don't give a damn about who gets hurt along the way . . . so long as they stay on the winning end. As if this place doesn't have enough suffering! The way I see it, that's simply making things worse by putting everyone against the corps, and it'll eventually bring its ruin. How can lawlessness be controlled if the ones who are supposedly the law enforcers are even more corrupt than the convicts?"

"For God's sake," Jim sighed, "sometimes I think you should have been a preacher. You sound too damned pious for your own good, Nick, and you'll get yourself in trouble every time if you spout off like that."

"Maybe," Nicholas chuckled. "But you know the saying, *do unto others* . . . blame it on my church schooling. Anyway, I reckon it would be best if I make the most of this opportunity. It might be my last one for a long time. And who knows, you might just be right when you say the same mistakes won't be made twice."

"Be that as it may . . . it's not this place that's got to you. It's Thornridge that's really put the wind up you."

"Yeah, and more than just a bit, but I wouldn't admit it to anyone else. I need to get out of here for more reasons than one . . . and the sooner the better."

"But is it wise to ship out? Isn't that running away? Why give Thornridge the satisfaction?"

"Because he's got a mind to kill me, and I'd rather keep my head than my dignity, thanks very much." Nicholas gave a half-hearted laugh trying to make light of the threat, but in truth, he was gravely concerned for his safety, knowing the baby could well be his. One way or another, he knew he had to get out of Sydney Town. Disliking the place as intensely as he did, there was certainly no incentive to make even a half-hearted attempt at bravery. No, he was going to shoot through, his hide and hair intact.

"Well, don't expect me to volunteer with you. I've got too good a thing going with Mary Kelly. When my land grant comes up, I'm going to petition the governor for permission to marry her. If she'll have me, that is."

For a few moments, Nicholas' woes evaporated, and he laughed again—this time meaning it. "Congratulations, mate. She'll have you all right. What woman wouldn't? Few men are as hard working. She'll consider you a fine catch, but I had no idea you were that serious, you sly old fox." A playful punch caught Jim's upper arm. "And I wouldn't expect you to volunteer just because I did."

"If you're still here for the wedding, I'll be asking you to stand up for me."

"It would be an honour." But Nicholas fully expected to be in Van Diemen's Land by the time Jim and Mary would be granted permission to marry and need a best man. Such things were never done in a hurry, protocol always protracting what appeared to be a simple request, and with the French eager to fly their flag over Van Diemen's Land, Governor King would no doubt hasten the departure of a British expedition down south.

Nicholas calculated Emmeline's baby would be due in six weeks, maybe a little longer if he was lucky, but with the knowledge that governmental processes rarely happen quickly, he feared the colonization expedition wouldn't be organised soon enough. If the baby arrived first, how was he going to avoid Thornridge until the ships set sail?

Would he even be accepted for the mission?

Chapter 5

Strained ropes creaked against the billowing sails as howling August winds propelled the full-rigged whaler through the waves. Fending off the icy spray with his collar drawn high around his neck, Nicholas dashed for the bulwark. Negotiating the rolling deck, he clung to the wooden railing and hung his head over the side as involuntary muscles attempted to empty his already hollow stomach into the merciless ocean below.

He had been one of the few men not to succumb to the clutches of seasickness during the voyage from England to New South Wales, so Nicholas was bewildered and vexed by this unpredicted response to the crossing of Bass Strait. Racked by nausea, feeling wretched and disgusting, he was powerless to do anything but wallow in infirmity and self-pity. Only the cabin boy, with his ladles of water to prevent dehydration, offered any sympathy or support.

Their ship, a small barque called the *Albion*, was a south-sea whaler that had been requested to carry the excess people and supplies that could not be accommodated on His Majesty's armed tender, *Lady Nelson*, which had been commissioned for the expedition. The ships encountered inclement weather soon after departure from Sydney's Port Jackson. There was one brief period of fine weather, but essentially the harrowing conditions over the past six days had buffeted the barque and all on board relentlessly, showing no consideration for the stomachs of convict or keeper.

Although the vessel cut a clean path through the heaving mountains of water, the rough passage took its toll on all except the most hardened of seafarers. But it was the animals that faired worst. Already three sheep and four lambs had been lost, and it looked as though one of the cows would also succumb. If the trend continued, the success of the settlement in Van Diemen's Land would be severely jeopardised. No one was entirely sure what the new land would offer. Although earlier reports spoke of tall trees and rolling pasture land, sources of abundant food found locally could not be relied upon. But one thing was certain. Without a good supply of livestock, the settlers would likely starve. Thus the animals were more important than settlers, with every effort made to ensure the remaining livestock stayed as healthy as possible. They were watched and attended to constantly, given fresh water and food, and kept clean and dry at all times.

Nicholas again retched bile and spittle into the sea, groaning with the violent spasms that rented his stomach to the point of rupture. Even the cabin boy's water refused to stay down.

Just when he thought he could take no more, the convulsions subsided and Nicholas hauled himself to the centre of the deck, where the motion of the vessel was less nauseating. He squatted on the sea-sprayed planks and wiped his face with a crinkly, well-used handkerchief, welcoming the fresh air despite the driving wind. He was exhausted, almost too debilitated to move, wishing the voyage would end. But no land was in sight, just mountains of slate-grey water capped by swirling foam in every direction, and the weather showed no sign of letting up. If it kept on like this, Nicholas doubted he would survive the distance, despite their destination on the Derwent River being only a matter of days away. His body craved nourishment, but the mere thought of food sent him rushing to the rails once more.

When the final wave of purging ceased, Nicholas staggered back to the merciful refuge at the centre of the deck. He felt so wretched he almost wished he was back in Sydney Town. Facing Thornridge seemed a better option at this point . . . almost. He'd managed to avoid the man after the tent incident and didn't know if Emmeline had given birth yet. Things had moved swiftly, with the organization of the colonization expedition well under way by the time the corps had even heard about it. Keen for volunteers, Nicholas was readily accepted. So here he was, not entirely sure his decision had been the right one after all.

Wet to the skin, he began to shake uncontrollably in the bone-chilling wind, the tremors assaulting his entire body. But it mattered little. Chattering teeth were preferable to continual heaving, so while the sails snapped and strained overhead, he chose to brave the iciness of the deck rather than endure the rigours of nausea and vomiting in the stuffiness, but relative warmth, of his quarters below.

Unfortunately, for the common corps members, their quarters were little better than the stifling hold that confined the convicts. Conditions were cramped and fresh air virtually nonexistent, rendering the entire area dank and squalid. None of the privates was particularly given to tidiness either. There was no sense complaining about what most agreed were appalling conditions because there was no possibility of relocation, every available space on board having been utilised for either storage or accommodation. Their only recompense was the fact the voyage was expected to be short, lasting around seven days, if all went well.

Within a few minutes Nicholas' violent shuddering and chattering teeth stopped along with the sickness. Numb to everything, he at last felt comfortable, peaceful. Lulled into a state of physical bliss, his worries and fears paled into nonexistence. This at last was the respite long sought. Nicholas closed his eyes and drifted to a place immune to the rampaging waves and quickly succumbed to oblivion.

Chapter 6

This particular voyage was in fact the second time the expedition had set sail for Van Diemen's Land. The first attempt, made earlier in August, was frustrated by even worse winds that forced the return of the ships to Sydney Town. At that point, Nicholas would have willingly withdrawn from the venture, plagued by apprehension and an ever-present gnawing fear of the unknown. There had even been talk that the *Porpoise*, originally commissioned to accompany the *Lady Nelson*, was something less than seaworthy, which did nothing to boost Nicholas' confidence. But the unforeseen delay in departure resulted in a change to the shipping plans, with the *Porpoise* being replaced by the much sturdier *Albion*, captained by Eber Bunker. Lieutenant Bowen must have entertained similar concerns because he subsequently decided to travel on the solid little whaler.

While the news of a sounder ship replenished his confidence, Nicholas found himself wishing he had never volunteered; however, to his surprise, several corps members started to regard him with awe, and he knew to recant would result in this newly acquired elevation in status quickly evaporating. Some corps men actually admitted he was far braver than they. Of course this didn't extend to Rogers and his cronies, who still considered volunteering to be stupid and akin to betrayal. In their eyes, true corps men never volunteered for anything unless there was a profit to be had. The mere thought of a reversion to their incessant ridicule if he changed his mind convinced Nicholas that Van Diemen's Land was the far better option. He could not stand being labelled the regiment's milksop all over again. It failed to enter his mind that permission to withdraw from the expedition at that point was not likely to be granted anyway. And there was always the threat from Thornridge.

Before the second departure, Captain Bunker, typical of any whaling captain, sought permission from Governor King to whale during the voyage if the opportunity presented itself. The request was granted, provided all convicts were confined and handcuffed until the chase boats returned to the *Albion*. So when the weather permitted, a watch was kept from the crow's nest, but for the most part, the seas were far too rough to have a man aloft on a swinging mast while the vessel plunged through mountainous seas. Even if a watch was mounted during the bleakest weather, chasing whales in small boats under such conditions was far too hazardous to contemplate, even for the bravest and most seasoned whalers.

Apart from the brief period of calm weather on the Friday following their departure, the bad weather that dogged the two ships for days on end resulted in the *Lady Nelson* going off on her own way. Nothing had been seen of her for several days, but the *Albion*, despite the endemic seasickness, was bearing up well under the adverse conditions. This was enhanced by the spirited Captain Bunker, who agreed to be part of the expedition for the payment of 204 pounds of tobacco, 336 pounds of old rope suitable for caulking, one pair of rudder chains, forty fathoms of three-inch worn rope, and one foresail. It was fine payment for such a short voyage, particularly when whaling was permitted. By his reckoning, there was nothing to lose and much to gain. The possibility of the ship foundering, which must have entered his mind when the barque was struck by the continual storms, appeared to do nothing to dampen his enthusiasm. Undoubtedly he had encountered numerous such storms during his many voyages across the Pacific Ocean, around Cape Horn, and in the Atlantic Ocean. Such men were not easily intimidated, especially with such a reward in sight.

But now, after days of confinement in abysmal conditions since leaving Port Jackson, everyone's nerves were a little frayed. Tensions mounted not only because of the confined space on the ship and the number of people on board, but also from the exasperation of unrelenting nausea which refused to subside.

Aside from the whaling crew, there were only forty-nine people, including Lieutenant Bowen and Doctor Mountgarrett, bound for Van Diemen's Land. Half of these were aboard the *Albion* with Nicholas. While the number was not considered excessive for a vessel the size of the *Albion* given the relatively short length of the voyage, most of the available space was taken up with supplies for the new settlement, including the livestock. All told, the vessel was crowded and, because of the bulky stores, was heavily laden. But this failed to deter an enthusiastic Captain Bunker from wanting to seize any opportunity to add to the load by harvesting the produce of any whale unfortunate enough to cross the ship's path. Perhaps he knew a whale chase was certain to relieve everyone's built-up tensions and boredom.

There was no way of knowing how long Nicholas had been asleep on the deck, but his welcomed inertia was roughly interrupted by someone tugging at his arm. Nicholas tried to ignore the irritating intruder. His efforts were unsuccessful, and through a deep, cavernous haze that all but sucked him back into unconsciousness, he discerned an earnest voice.

"Ya cain't stay here, matey; ya'll freeze to death." It was Buck, one of the two American whalers from Nantucket, and the only black man to form part of Bunker's crew. He was older than the others, stronger, and with vastly more experience. "Get ta ya feet now, an' I'll help ya below."

"I'll die if I go down there," Nicholas half whispered in his stupor, all the time trying to wrestle his arm free.

"Ya'll die, sure as the sun sets, if'n ya stay 'ere, Nicky, me lad. Come on, up ya get. Quick now. Don't ya be fight'n it, 'cause I'll carry ya if'n I has ta," came Buck's gruff command as he persisted in his efforts to drag Nicholas to his feet.

"No," Nicholas protested feebly. "I don't feel half as bad here. Leave me be, Buck."

"An' well that may be, lad, but ya'll be dead by nightfall in this weather if'n ya stays 'ere. Ya has ta get some warmth inta ya bones."

"But I don't feel so cold now. I'm all right. Really."

"That's cos ya's numb all over from bein' wet thru an' sittin' in this 'ere wind. Ya stays 'ere, lad, an' ya won't be feelin' nothin' ever agin. Ya understand me?"

Somewhere in Nicholas' clouded consciousness the reality of the words struck home. Maybe he wasn't ready to die yet. Nodding in agreement, he tried to get to his feet, but was pulled up short by pain in the tendons behind his cold-stiffened knees, which refused to straighten. With a moan of agony, he collapsed back onto the deck.

"So ya's not so numb after all," Buck grinned, hauling him up in his brawny arms and carrying him toward the hatch. "That's a good sign, ol' son. Ya'll mend a'right with a bit o' heat on ya."

Nicholas was unconvinced; surely he was going to die . . . and it didn't seem to matter anymore.

Chapter 7

Within minutes, Nicholas was stripped of his sodden clothing, wrapped in a wad of thick blankets, placed on his bunk, and able to tolerate a little water before the teeth-chattering shivers resumed.

"That's another good sign, lad. The rattles 'll help ya warm up then they'll settle and ya'll be a'right," reassured Buck. "Ya rest, now, an' don't go roamin' out on deck in this weather agin. Use that there bucket if'n ya must. That's what it's furr." He turned for the door.

Nicholas hadn't experienced such kindness in a long time, except of course from Jim who was far behind in Sydney Town, eagerly awaiting his approaching marriage. Since their paths were unlikely to cross again, he appreciated a new friend in Buck, even if he too would ultimately go with the eventual departure of the *Albion* from Van Diemen's Land when she set sail in her never-ending quest for the whale.

Nicholas watched Buck striding across the room, his dark skin blending into the sienna-shadowed surrounds. The two of them had hit it off from the first meeting, but they were worlds apart in age, background, and experience. He was more than twice Nicholas' age, a freed slave from Virginia, who'd scraped a living doing whatever he could as he made his way north. Later he married a good woman whom he lost through the complications of childbirth the same year. When he obtained solid work on a ship operating out of Rhode Island, he was forced to leave his young son with his dead wife's relatives, sending them money for the child's upkeep and education regularly. Eventually, because there was more money to be had from whaling, he found his way to Nantucket Island and wound up making a living from the slaughter of whales. Life had been hard for Buck, and yet he was a good, kind man—someone you could always count on. His son, now running a meagre business and raising a family of his own in Providence, gave evidence to that.

"Hey, Buck, I owe you," Nicholas stammered, trying unsuccessfully to check his violent shuddering.

The huge man turned. "Couldn't leave ya out there ta die, now could I? Ya's a'right, Nicky, me lad. Keep ya nose clean an' ya should do good in this new place ya's goin to, just like I did in Nantucket." He grinned, revealing the now familiar mass of crooked white teeth, which were far beyond help. "Not many black men get ta do whaling. I was lucky. I's got a good life, and so has m' boy. Ya can do it too. Now, I's got ta be goin' cos thar's work ta be done."

Buck disappeared, and just as he predicted, Nicholas' shivering subsided. It wasn't long before the wretched nausea ceased and welcome calmness enveloped him, allowing him to slip into a sleep such as he had not enjoyed for days.

The following morning, the seventh day of the voyage, brought a period of fair weather. Nicholas felt much better and was able to down a hearty breakfast, as did most people on board. Later, nearly everyone was on deck enjoying the welcome sunshine. Both convicts and guards alike were lazily sunning themselves in a gentle breeze when a cry from the crow's nest high above pierced the serenity.

"Thar she blows!"

Instantly the crew and the corps sprang into action. Convicts were hustled below to the confines of their hold while three whaleboats, each around twenty-five-feet long and carrying six men—a boat head and five rowers—were quickly lowered into the water. The boat head of the leading vessel, who was also the first mate, sat at the stern to steer the boat while Buck, the harpooner, sat nearest the bow, helping the remaining men row.

On the *Albion's* deck, Nicholas strained to see any sign of the source of the excitement. The water was a clear, cobalt blue, broken only by streaks of white foam. Scanning the ocean, at first he saw nothing, then following the direction of the outstretched arm of the overhead lookout, he spotted the tell-tale spouts of white water shooting high into the air several hundred yards off to starboard. There appeared to be three of them: huge, dark-gray things some sixty feet in length. Nicholas had never seen anything like them, not even on his first voyage. They were magnificent, their bodies massive, with enormous heads containing the sought-after reservoir of spermaceti taking up approximately one third of their body length.

Nicholas watched their every move, mesmerised. The whales ploughed lazily through the water, breaching regularly to breathe. He could hear the low, moisture-laden whoosh of the creatures exhaling, sending white, foamy water streaking high into the sky before their blowholes closed, and they plunged again, aided by the slap of their mighty flat tails on the surface as they did so. They were the most powerful, yet serenely peaceful creatures Nicholas had ever seen, and he felt a sense of dread as the three boats, their teams ready, stealthily approached them.

The men rowed in silence to avoid the whales detecting unfamiliar sounds and be startled into action before Buck had a chance to drive his harpoon home. If the whales moved off at speed and a long chase ensued, Nicholas knew from what Buck had told him, the boat head would give the order to hoist a sail, allowing a much more silent approach, which would give the men a chance to rest from rowing.

The lead boat neared the closest whale, the craft less than a third of the creature's size. Buck rose, holding his weapon ready. The woman beside Nicholas gasped. It was Eliza Edwards, pregnant wife of one of the corps members, and whether her reaction was one of horror or exhilaration, he did not know or care; his eyes were riveted firmly on Buck. The harpoon, measuring about eight feet in length from its sharp, barbed, steel point to the end of its wooden pole, had a long rope attached to its end, which was fastened to a post in the stern where the remainder of the line lay coiled in a large tub.

Nicholas watched as the boats avoided the closest whale, heading instead for the larger one in the middle. Buck waited until the boat almost touched the whale—*wood to black skin*, he had called it. Then he threw the harpoon with all his strength deep into the side of the huge beast. Instantly the whale surged forward, and the line trailed smoke as it uncoiled and sped around the boat's stocky wooden peg used to slow the whale's pace by providing tension. To prevent the line bursting into flame, the peg was cooled by repeated dousing with water as the whale lunged forward, taking the little boat for a sleigh ride. Such rides could last for hours, the boat bouncing along behind the wounded creature in a shower of spray.

After being harpooned most whales either sounded, diving to the depths of the ocean, or swam off at high speed in an attempt to outrun their attackers. Some whales, particularly the sperm variety, turned and attacked the boat instead. One blow from the whale's immense tail could smash a boat to splinters. Many whalers lost their lives that way. Alternatively, if the whale sounded too deeply, and the crew was unable to cut the rope in time, the whale would drag the boat down into the depths, often drowning all on board.

The remaining two whales remained oblivious to the plight of their companion, giving the other boats time to advance close enough to gouge their harpoons deep into the defenceless flesh. Then the chase was on. All three boats bounced south across the waves in a hail of spray, behind panic-stricken whales fleeing for their lives, with the *Albion* in hot pursuit of all. Most of those on board had never seen the like and scrambled around each other along the railing to gain the best vantage point. Nicholas was in the thick of it, not because he liked what he saw, but more a morbid fascination with the battle of strength and wills between whale and whaler. If size was any indication, the whales should prevail, but the intellect and tenacity of meagre men mostly rendered them the victors.

The contest lasted for hours, and the audience's interest eventually waned with people drifting off in pursuit of other activities, returning only occasionally to keep abreast of any new development. Nicholas was one of the few who remained steadfast at the bow observing the whole event. Once, when the whaleboats were vertically suspended for a moment after striking an unusually large wave, he feared Buck would be thrown into the water, but the man's experience and dexterity kept him on board. Many such incidents followed, and it became apparent such hair-raising buffeting was merely part of it all.

Finally, after several hours of dragging the boats through the waves, the whales tired, and the men, heaving on the ropes, brought their boats close to the massive, ailing beasts. Nicholas watched as one by one the boat heads lanced the whales' huge sides, piercing their lungs, with long iron blades. Blood gushed into the water, turning it crimson, and the men were similarly stained as blood sprayed from the creatures' blowholes during their final, dying gasps. The once magnificent beasts of the sea quickly bled to death as the exhausted, but gratified men watched on, impervious to the whales' mournful demise.

The sight sickened Nicholas. The smell of blood filled his nostrils, and he could almost taste its metallic tang as two of the dead whales were towed back to the ship and tied alongside, one starboard, the other to port. The waves washed over the immense carcasses, sweeping more blood into the water, and the *Albion* was enveloped in a sea of red. Using spade-like knives on long poles, the blood-covered whalers clambered onto the lifeless carcasses, peeling off the creatures' blubber in two long, spiral strips, slowing rolling them over and over in the water. It reminded Nicholas of paring an orange.

Attracted by the blood, dozens of sharks of all sizes came to assist in the whales' dissection, ripping mouthfuls of flesh from the now almost unrecognisable creatures. Unable to turn away, Nicholas stood riveted, yet horrified, until the spiral blubber strips were long enough for the loose ends to be dragged aboard and cut into smaller sections called blanket strips.

At this point, most of the women were too repulsed to watch any further and disappeared below deck. Nicholas had the same urge, but not wanting to be perhaps considered cowardly, he gritted his teeth and steeled his stomach against the abhorrent onslaught to his senses. No one was ever going to be given a reason to label him a milksop again. Not ever. But the whole vile procedure appalled him to the core.

The deck was soon awash with blood as the blanket strips were chopped into block-shaped pieces and these in turn reduced to bacon-like slices called bible leaves. The latter would be kept for the cooking process: *trying out*, Buck called it, during which the valuable oil was extracted. Because sperm whales had teeth, there were no long plates of baleen to be hacked from the creature's mouth, so the whalers busied themselves extracting the spermaceti from its head and preparing to examine the intestines for ambergris. In Europe, spermaceti was used in the manufacture of cosmetics and ambergris as a stabiliser in perfume. Cosmetic houses always paid a good price for such commodities.

The men still standing on the carcasses proceeded to remove the bulky, unwieldy bowel of each whale through a deep, gaping hole cut on the underside of each creature and sited well out of reach of the marauding sharks. The gut was then carefully inspected for any solid mass that could be ambergris. When the first chunk was hacked free and hoisted on deck, its extremely repugnant smell brought handkerchiefs and coat sleeves to the noses of most spectators as they hastily shuffled backward.

Again Nicholas' stomach turned, as did everyone's, and he

thought it amazing how such a repulsive, stinking substance could somehow develop such a pleasant, sweet, musty odour following prolonged contact with air and could be used successfully in perfume. It occurred to him that if women were to witness its extraction, they would probably think twice about wearing their fragrances.

Last of all, the whales' huge teeth were prised from their immense, flaccid jaws so the whalers could while away their idle time carving intricate pictures onto them, the saleable end product, known as scrimshaw, adding to their income. Buck, who turned out to be quite an artist, had many elaborately carved specimens, all of which were his personal favourites. When Nicholas was shown the collection he was fascinated with the art and offered to buy one, but Buck was reluctant to part with any, saying if he had a mind to sell his special collection he could get a better price elsewhere. It seemed they were greatly prized in certain parts of the world, not only for their art, but for the mythical properties they were said to possess and the fact that they were hard to come by.

After all the blubber, spermaceti, ambergris, and teeth were harvested the remnants of the whales' bodies, having no further use, were cut loose for the frenzied sharks. Then the last remaining whale was brought alongside and the whole process repeated.

But that was not the end of it.

The blubbery bible leaves had yet to be tried out in huge iron try-pots, blackened by a lifetime of sitting over roaring fires, while their pulpy content was transformed into the prized liquid oil.

During the trying out period, the *Albion* lay anchored for three days in Oyster Bay on the east coast of Van Diemen's

Land. It was a picturesque spot, every bit as rugged as New South Wales, perhaps even more so, and the familiarity fired Nicholas with enthusiasm. Again he looked forward to the challenge of establishing a new colony, and as Buck suggested, he would work hard, stay out of trouble, and do well in the land that time overlooked.

Even the occasional sighting of groups of aborigines along the coastline did nothing to quell his excitement. Some of the more experienced corps members, remembering previous skirmishes in New South Wales, feared an attack and became quite agitated at the sight of their ebony frames on the hillside and lurking in the scrub just beyond the beach. But although the natives watched the newcomers' every move, there was no sign of hostility or aggression, only curiosity, and when no contact was attempted by either party, they retreated further back into the scrub and out of sight. The crew continued peacefully with the business of gathering timber and stoking the blazing inferno under the try-pots while the blubber percolated.

But it did not sit well in the minds of many that they were continually being watched by unseen eyes.

Chapter 8

Lieutenant Bowen surveyed the sinister crags of the coastline through his spyglass as the *Albion* rounded the lofty cliffs of Cape Raoul and entered Storm Bay on the second Saturday of September 1803. A scowl creased his fresh young features. What he saw reminded him a little of Norfolk Island, but these cliffs were higher and more rugged, rendering the cape that much more intimidating.

The sheer beauty of the area made Bowen wonder if it was this alone that enticed Bass and Flinders south for a second time to further their explorations, eventually proving Van Diemen's Land was an island separated from mainland Australia by a deep channel, which they named Bass Strait.

Governor King's instructions to Bowen were simple: establish the new colony somewhere along the shores of the Derwent River, which the map indicated flowed into the northwest side of Storm Bay. By all accounts, an appropriate site for the new township would not be difficult to locate. Had it not been for the numerous streams and grasslands charted by previous surveyors, Bowen would have been extremely anxious in the face of such towering cliffs, but because of good maps, he was confident in finding many suitable places only a short distance upstream from the mouth of the river.

Over the years, numerous surveys of varying scope had been conducted in the area, the first by the Dutch explorer, Abel Janszoon Tasman, who'd named the island Van Diemen's Land after the then-governor-general of Batavia. The land then lay undisturbed for one hundred and fifty years, apparently forgotten, until visited by rival French and British explorers. As a result, Bowen could now call upon their cumulative mapping efforts.

The Derwent received its name from the English captain, John Hayes, who sailed partially up its waters and thought to name it after the beautiful river of the same name in Cumberland. From this, Bowen deduced the river must be extremely picturesque.

Even William Bligh, captain of the *Bounty*, visited Van Diemen's Land on his way to Tahiti, returning four years and one mutiny later, when he attempted to improve the island's food supply by planting several fruit trees, acorns, and vegetables. Lieutenant Bowen hoped that some of Bligh's legacy had survived the harsh climate and could be utilised by the new settlers. When they disembarked, and after their immediate needs of shelter and security were met, he planned to send a small exploratory party in search of Bligh's fruit and vegetables. This group would be charged with exploring the inland area, recording its topography, and keeping an eye out for any natural resources beneficial to the colony.

While the sturdy whaler, under full sail and in fair weather, cut its path swiftly through the currents of Storm Bay heading northwest toward the mouth of the Derwent, Captain John Bowen dwelt little on the island's brief history. He was only minimally aware he was about to add another chapter to its chronicle, his immediate concern being to locate their accompanying vessel, the *Lady Nelson*. What fate had befallen her since encountering the gales over a week ago he knew not.

The same question was on Nicholas' mind when, from his position at the stern of the ship, he observed the huge expanse of the bay and saw no sign of the *Lady Nelson*.

"Maybe she's foundered in them storms," offered Buck, his huge frame supported by the taut rigging he was lazily draped across.

"Possibly," Nicholas replied, shading his eyes from the sun. "But wouldn't we have seen wreckage?"

"Nah, could be washed off anywheres, especially near the strait. Currents is real strong there, 'n besides, we might'a been in front when she went down. Wouldn't see nothin' then. Slip straight to the bottom in our wake, she would."

If Captain Courtoys and the *Lady Nelson* were lost along with half their stores and supplies, there would be hard times ahead for the few who would remain behind in Van Diemen's Land after the *Albion* set sail again. They had carried enough stores and supplies to last eight months, but after the bad weather, much of it had been damaged or spoiled. So, without the Lady Nelson's contribution, there would be limited equipment to build a storehouse to protect what remained, not to mention shelters to house everyone. Food would have to be severely rationed if they were to survive.

As darkness fell and the *Albion* found safe anchorage in a small bay, their future prospects were uncertain. An anxious, if quiet night, was had by all. Only the night watchman and a fretful Lieutenant Bowen remained awake long after midnight, wondering what misfortune had befallen the *Lady Nelson* and what their own future held.

Chapter 9

The next morning, much to everyone's relief, but particularly Lieutenant Bowen's, the *Albion* sailed into the Derwent to find the *Lady Nelson* patiently awaiting their arrival. The armed brig lay anchored in Risdon Cove on the eastern bank, having arrived five days earlier without mishap.

Fortunately the soldiers and convicts on both ships arrived in good health, although Captain Courtoys reported the health of some of the *Lady Nelson*'s crew to be a little wanting. Likewise, the cattle did not fare well under the battering gales and were bruised so badly they lost one cow, three sheep, and four lambs from the general supply, as well as much more personal stock belonging to Lieutenant Bowen and the settlers. Bowen was particularly displeased because half of his stock had succumbed, but at least most of the stores were intact. With a bit of effort by all, once the site for the settlement was chosen, shelters could be raised quickly and then gardens prepared in readiness for the sowing of vegetables and grain.

A perplexed Bowen surveyed the banks on both sides of the river, uncertain in his decision as to the most suitable place to settle. After discounting many promising sites, he eventually chose to remain right where they were, at Risdon Cove, because there was a creek delivering a much better stream of fresh water to the Derwent than that found at any other site. Not only was it the most convenient, he considered it also the most appropriate, and immediately gave the order to disembark all the stores as well as the colonists. The latter comprised a detachment of the New South Wales Corps, including one lance-sergeant and seven privates, who were accompanied by four women and one child. The remainder were James Smith, who had recently been made convict overseer by Bowen; Thomas Wilson, the storekeeper; and twenty-one male and three female convicts.

The last to disembark were the free settlers. Mr. and Mrs. John Clarke, Mr. and Mrs. Leo Turner, and Mr. and Mrs. Walter Burton and their two children—all pleased to have their feet again on dry land—immediately set about securing themselves against the weather. In doing so they discovered, much to Bowen's delight, extensive valleys to the back of the cove. He then directed the settlement be situated on the nearest hill, a good choice in his opinion because it commanded an excellent view of the river and surrounding land. Given the good soil and the babbling stream, Risdon Cove offered everything necessary for the success of the colony. Bowen was more than content with his selection.

Nicholas, along with the other soldiers who were not directly supervising convicts, busied themselves erecting temporary shelters for themselves and Lieutenant Bowen, whose permanent hut was to be constructed adjacent to the site of the proposed garden on the hilltop.

Bowen's hut was also intended to house his lady friend, Martha Hayes, who had accompanied him on the voyage. Little had been seen of her so far, since she had mostly remained below deck in the cabin she shared with Bowen, probably due to the bad weather and sea sickness. Those who did happen to see the young Miss Hayes commented on her beauty and wondered why the lieutenant governor hadn't made an honourable woman of her. Although it was not uncommon for men in service to take a mistress, it became the subject of jokes and was widely discussed by crew and corps.

Beyond the garden, further over the hill, three huts to be barracks for the detachment of the corps were to be built. Between them and the creek, it was proposed to house the convicts. Further inland, where the stream carved a path to the north, Bowen allotted five acres of land each to the settlers Walter Burton, Leo Turner, and John Clarke, and also to Jacob Mountgarrett, the surgeon, who were all keen to complete the construction of their accommodations in the shortest time possible.

It was the convicts who first drove Bowen and the soldiers close to despair. Aside from none of them being even slightly inclined to work, their ranks held no true craftsmen or artisans. Even the blacksmith had no idea how to forge nails, leading Bowen to fear the settlement would fall short of them, particularly spike nails used in heavy construction.

"What do you mean you can't make nails?" Bowen challenged the blacksmith, Owen Rhodes, who was escorted to his tent by Overseer Smith.

"That's just it, Cap'n, sir. I cain't make 'em."

"Isn't that quite remarkable for a blacksmith?" Bowen eyed the man severely, convinced he was lying.

"I was only ever apprentice, Cap'n. Never learned t' make nails."

"I would have thought forging nails would be one of the first things an apprentice blacksmith would learn," Bowen retorted.

"No, sir. Never learned how." The blacksmith was polite, but sullen, steadfast in his resolve not to make nails for his captors, no matter how he was pressed.

"Then just what did you learn?"

"I dunno. Lots of things." He glared defiantly at Lieutenant Bowen. "Blacksmith things, sir. You wouldn't understand."

"Try me, Mr. Rhodes, and kindly be specific."

"Well, let's see." The man stroked his chin, feigning memory loss, which did nothing to improve Bowen's waning patience. "How to work the bellows so's fire's hot enough, how t' melt metal, t' make horseshoes . . ."

"But not nails?"

"No, sir, not nails."

"Mr. Rhodes," menaced Bowen, "I am suggesting to you that you do indeed have a knowledge of forging nails, and I further put it to you that you will remember how this task is performed in the very near future. Failing that, the lash may refresh your memory." Then abruptly turning to Smith, he said, "Get him out of here."

"It aint a case of rememberin', sir," Rhodes protested feebly, a satisfied smirk on his face as he was escorted from the tent. "Like I said, don't know how t' make 'em."

Bowen was wise to the man's deception, but had no way of proving it, and while ever there was doubt in his mind, Rhodes knew he would not be flogged. But even if Bowen was not true to character and decided to order the flogging, it was still not going to produce the nails he so desperately wanted.

Rhodes was greeted with nothing but praise from his fellow

convicts once the story of his interrogation by Bowen was relayed, albeit with much exaggeration.

"Good on yer, mate. Showed him a thing or two."

"Young upstart's not goin' to push us around."

"If 'e tries, we'll just stick together. There's strength in numbers. He'll never get the better of us then. Mark me words."

Nicholas, outside on guard duty, overheard their entire conversation and was not surprised. He knew convicts in New South Wales rarely cooperated with the authorities, so why should it be any different here? Nevertheless, he decided to report what he'd heard the following day, but had little confidence anything would, or could, be done to change the situation with the nails.

Convict attitude to work changed only minimally after Lieutenant Bowen made it quite clear that, without their cooperation, they would have no weatherproof shelters and would be placed on reduced rations when current supplies became depleted, owing to their inability to produce for their own needs.

Acutely aware he and the convicts held different priorities, Bowen knew there would be no cooperation if the task at hand was for the betterment of the settlement, but if their comfort and privileges were threatened they would soon see things differently. When faced with the prospect of hunger and physical discomfort, even the most recalcitrant of felons decided it was in his own best interest to start felling trees and clearing the land so a vegetable garden could be prepared and so there would be building material for the huts. But they did so amid much sullenness and endless grumbling.

The crude housing they eventually constructed consisted

basically of four walls made of interlaced tree branches, mostly wattle, smeared on both sides with generous amounts of clay to render a smooth surface inside and out. Once dry, the clay provided shelter from all but the fiercest of winds, and a solidly thatched roof kept the inhabitants dry when it rained. The result satisfied the querulously indolent convicts, who then again displayed their unwillingness to toil at the government garden or at any other task allotted by Overseer Smith or an increasingly exasperated Captain John Bowen.

Setbacks were inevitable, which made Bowen appreciate all the more any small bonus which came his way, the first being an offer by settler John Clarke, a retired soldier of the corps and one-time stonemason, to build a solid stone storehouse to accommodate the government stores. He said it would take him less than one month, and Clarke's only condition was to be granted one man to assist during the construction. Naturally, Bowen eagerly agreed to the proposal.

Accommodating the settlement's provisions and food supplies was high on the list of Bowen's priorities. Most of these had survived the voyage almost intact, with the exception of a little damaged sugar and flour, and required secure dry storage. Since there was an ample supply of easily quarried sandstone in a nearby hill, Bowen's intention was to have numerous stone buildings constructed in the future, his own house included.

But there was much more for Bowen to consider. After taking the necessary measures to secure his charges, clear the land, and make preparation for cultivation, Governor King had requested that Bowen assess the prospects of future farming, grazing, and logging. Of particular interest was whether the available timber was of sufficient quality and quantity to be viably transported back to England for ship construction.

After that, there were the climatic observations. Here, he was to record the prevailing seasonal winds, the rise and fall of the tides, and the start and end of the dry and rainy seasons. All this, while ensuring law and order was maintained, Sunday services were conducted according to the Church of England, and the settlement became self-sufficient in the shortest time possible.

Convicts, being servants of the Crown, were supposed to labour from daylight to dusk, allowing one hour for breakfast and two hours for the midday meal, and their food rations were to consist of four pounds of pork and seven pounds of biscuits per week unless supplies were depleted. New suits, or slops, as they were generally known, were to be issued to all convicts twice each year, in December and June. Bowen was fully aware of his power to deny his charges their privileges in order to get them to work. And work, they must. It was a tactic he didn't want to resort to, but he certainly would . . . if he had to.

To retain the security required of a penal colony, King had charged Bowen with maintaining a closed port to all vessels, except those in distress, and to deny permission for the building of any vessel exceeding twenty feet in keel. Too many vessels in port, especially those that could be used for longer voyages, increased the likelihood of convict escape by water. If such vessels were simply not available, there could be no escapes except by land—and that was considered highly improbable because there was nowhere to go except inland, where the land was often rugged and held the possibility of aboriginal attack.

But closed port or not, convict idleness, Bowen knew all too well, was the devil's workshop, resulting in collusion and attempts to escape.

Chapter 10

With the departure of the *Albion* the next day, there would be only one ship left in the Derwent, leaving the settlement's complete isolation one step closer. The notion unexpectedly left Nicholas with an uneasy, queasy feeling similar to what he experienced when he first left his family and later his mate, Jim Hall, who became like family. Only a few affected him this way . . . their absence from his life so absolute, his sadness leaving him hollow. Now he could add Buck Jones to the list.

If things were different, Nicholas may have agreed to Buck's suggestion that he join him in Nantucket and become a whaler when his time in the corps ended, but Nicholas was attracted to the farming life he was more familiar with, and if things turned out well for him in Van Diemen's Land, he might apply for a fifty-acre land grant after his three-year stint was over instead of returning to England. Besides, he really had no taste for the harpoon. Buck accepted this without question, sensing his repulsion, and agreed it was not for everyone.

"I's not much fer writin', but m'be this will help ya remember me once 'n a while."

The cool, smooth object Buck thrust at him was a hand-carved piece of scrimshaw, its intricate design suggesting it had taken Buck many hours to complete. One side of the tooth carried an engraving of a whaler lying at anchor in what looked like Storm Bay and had a small inset picture of the carver. The other side displayed a likeness to Nicholas. Obviously it wasn't a part of the collection previously shown to him by Buck, so Nicholas knew it had been carved recently, especially for him.

"I'll keep it with me always, Buck." Nicholas smiled, taking his outstretched hand in a solid, vigorous shake. "And I'm not likely to ever forget the person who saved my life."

"Jist make sure it was one worth savin', tha's all I be askin'." With a final grin, the huge man splashed his way through the shallows toward the small boat waiting to ferry the last of the *Albion's* crew out to the deeper water where she lay in readiness.

"Look me up if you ever get back to these parts," Nicholas called after him, but there was no reply, his words swamped by distance and the splash of water.

Nicholas knew he would never forget this man. What he taught him and the kindness he had shown would stay with Nicholas for the remainder of his life, as would the whale's tooth he now shoved firmly into his pocket. There should be more men like Buck Jones, men with wisdom, dignity, and compassion, but it took a hard life to acquire such attributes, as Buck's story gave testimony.

Nicholas watched the oarsmen heave the little craft swiftly across the cove and raised his arm in one last farewell, almost oblivious to the movement of the small group gathered nearby to also bid the ship goodbye. He then trudged up the hill to the barracks from where he could watch the *Albion* slip down the Derwent and disappear into Storm Bay.

Buck had no propensity for long goodbyes. "Go quickly and never look back," were the words he always imparted to his son, for there was no sense in prolonging an inevitable parting. Yet when the ship was a good way downstream, he turned back toward the settlement and thought he could pick out Nick making his way slowly up the hill, but he couldn't be sure. They all looked alike in their red jackets. He was a good bloke, Buck thought, and if their paths should ever cross again, he, for one, wouldn't mind in the least. It was only when the settlement receded to a distant blur that Buck turned his attention to the mundane business of the manual tasks allocated him.

Meanwhile, Lieutenant Bowen sat outside his hut content at being able to have the *Albion* carry a short dispatch outlining the initial progress of the settlement to Governor King. He was confident King would be pleased with his efforts to date and would agree to provide further supplies, experienced tradesmen, and a motivated sergeant. The present incumbent impressed him little, often seeming almost as indolent as the convicts in his charge and frequently complaining that the work was too arduous or the guard difficult to mount. As far as Bowen was concerned, the soldiers were a very disgruntled lot who made it obvious they were used to a much easier life. When Bowen ordered the posting of one sentry on day duty and two at night, believing this was both adequate and reasonable guard duty, the soldiers did nothing but complain, considered it extremely burdensome and far beyond what was necessary.

Then there was the problem of insufficient food stores. Bowen intended to return the storm-damaged sugar and flour, along with a request for replacements, on the *Lady Nelson* when she set sail for New South Wales in another two weeks. His decision caused much grumbling by soldiers who failed to understand the reason for not sending it back on the *Albion*, which would have facilitated quicker replacement.

Resolute in his judgment, Bowen considered it was more appropriate to return the damaged stores at the same time as he planned to furnish Governor King with a far more detailed description of the settlement he now intended to name Hobart, after Lord Robert Hobart-Hampden, secretary for the Colonies. The governor would be more inclined to grant his request for replacements once he was convinced of the settlement's progress, especially if his report was accompanied by a precise map and details of his future plans for the infant township. Being mindful of the significant requests sent with the *Albion*, and not wishing to overtax the governor's generosity, Bowen thought this approach would meet with success. The governor would probably have already dispatched the items of his earlier request by the time he received an appeal for the replacement of the damaged flour and sugar . . . and the governor could hardly deny stores to a hungry colony.

Once the *Albion* was out of view, Bowen turned his attention to the budding little town on the hillside slopes and felt satisfied with what he saw. He'd placed the settlers' five acres about a quarter of a mile inland from his hut, near an ample supply of fresh water, but had not drawn up lines for the town immediately, preferring to await the felling of the tall trees so his view would be unobstructed.

His patience paid off.

Now the rudiments of the town were clearly laid down and the soldiers and prisoners had very comfortable huts and, as far as he was concerned, had no reason to complain. This left him free to pursue the other tasks the governor had given him: exploration and assessment of the area's likely produce.

Opposite Risdon Cove, he had noticed a fine inlet with deep water, the largest on the Derwent, which had been little noted on any of the charts available to him. Captain Courtoys had informed him earlier of another cove known as Ralph's Bay, which was very shallow and inaccurately charted. The *Lady Nelson* had grounded some distance from the shore on arrival, but luckily the vessel had easily moved off with the incoming tide. Bowen had been pleased to hear from Courtoys that flax plants were growing quite profusely in this particular bay, and he proposed to investigate its quality and whether it could be used for making storage bags, rope, and similar commodities the settlement would need. Bowen had also observed an abundant supply of wood in the area, including blue gum, she-oak, stringy bark, and mahogany, ensuring a future productive timber industry.

Only days after the departure of the *Albion*, Lieutenant Bowen, on his quest to fully explore the area, decided to venture up river to probe beyond the point where Captain Flinders had called a halt two years previously. He wanted to be the one to find the Derwent's source.

When Nicholas caught wind of Bowen's plan to explore the upper reaches of the Derwent, his imagination was captured and he decided to do whatever it took for him to be included in the venture.

Chapter 11

Bowen strode confidently down the hill, his shiny, black boots scattering beads of early morning dew. The previous day he had chosen two soldiers to accompany him up the Derwent, but was not entirely convinced as to their ability.

"Good morning, sir," Nicholas greeted the captain, his cheeks reddened more by enthusiasm than the cool air.

A distracted Bowen grunted a barely audible reply. It was with reluctance he was leaving his inept lance-sergeant in charge, but because there was no one else of higher rank, he had no choice. His comfort lay in the fact that he had convinced himself that little could possibly go wrong in the short time he proposed to be away.

Smith, already in the longboat, kept it trim as Bowen, then Nicholas, stepped aboard. One deft shove with an oar by the latter sent the craft smoothly into deeper water with an arc of silent ripples in its wake. The two soldiers then quickly took up their rowing positions as Bowen settled comfortably at the bow.

Nicholas had lied about his rowing proficiency in order to gain selection for the mission, and now he struggled to conceal his inadequacy. It was far more difficult than he imagined. He expected his back to ache, but not his thighs. Nor had he expected the well-worn wooden handles to torment his flesh as they did. Only sheer determination kept him going, and he was thankful Bowen was too busy surveying the shore and conferring with his map to be concerned about his rowers. Eventually Nicholas found Smith's rhythm and, numbing himself to the pain, stroke for stroke they hauled the heavy craft upstream in unison.

About six miles from Risdon Cove, the riverbanks became thickly wooded, obscuring the inland view, but beyond the place called Herdsman's Cove, the land levelled out. The riverbanks looked more like a nobleman's park in England than a wild, uncultivated country, and in every direction, they saw beautiful green pastureland.

A satisfied smile crossed Bowen's face. It would take very little effort to clear most of the valley for agriculture and farming. Nicholas was also thinking it would be an excellent place for a farm—maybe his own one day.

At one stage Bowen glimpsed aborigines moving about in a patch of scrub some fifty yards from the east bank, but by the time he raised his spyglass, they had vanished. As the rowers remained oblivious, Bowen thought perhaps it was his imagination. He had not seen a single native during the first few weeks of their arrival in Van Diemen's Land, yet some of the settlers reported sighting them fairly regularly in the valley beyond Risdon Cove. Apparently very shy, they made no attempt to approach the settlement. Bowen had an uneasy feeling about them, suspecting they were always in the background keeping the newcomers under close surveillance, but since they seemed to pose no threat and he considered them of little use, he made no effort to locate them. To his mind, the settlement was far better off without any contact.

So long as there remained no menace from the aborigines, Herdsman's Cove, in Bowen's view, would make an excellent spot for future settlers and, after scooping and gulping from his cupped hand, was pleased to discover the Derwent's water was perfectly fresh above it. There were very few rocky spots, except on the high hills, and because the land was flat and clear of trees or scrub in many places, a plough could be used immediately. Ruefully, Bowen considered the sad fact that he could easily employ one hundred men on the land if only he had them.

His thoughts turned to Private Nicholas Thomas, whose effort to master the oar and his obvious determination had not gone unnoticed. Recalling the report the young man had furnished concerning the convicts' boasting about their avoidance of nail making, Bowen had already concluded he was a soldier of worth—someone to be trusted. What's more, he could read and write, skills not found frequently in corps men.

Armed with Private Thomas' information, Bowen had greater understanding of just how hard-pushed he was really going to be in gaining the slightest amount of convict cooperation. He wished for more good soldiers like Private Thomas—keen men who wanted to do well. With more such men, the settlement would soon be a flourishing colony, but the pitiful lot of workmen at his disposal were far too few and decidedly disinclined to exert themselves.

Beyond Herdsman's Cove, the Derwent's flow slowed considerably, the river widening and becoming so shallow as to make shipping difficult. At this point, and with no desire to camp out overnight, Bowen ordered their return, satisfied the source of the Derwent lay just ahead and he could undoubtedly put a surveyor to good use in this rich valley.

During the return trip Bowen relaxed, settled back to take in the scenery and gave thought as to how he could best utilize the eager Private Thomas.

Chapter 12

It was late October. Bowen sat outside his quarters and followed the progress of two ships as they tacked slowly up the Derwent. It seemed his prayers for a few good men were finally about to be answered.

"The brig is the *Dart*," Bowen informed his assistant, unsuccessfully concealing his excitement. "And the schooner is the *Endeavour*. They'll drop anchor soon. Kindly prepare for their welcome, Mr. Little. They'll no doubt be carrying food supplies and more convicts so you'd best inform the storeman and Overseer Smith to make ready as well."

"Right away, Cap'n, sir," Bill Little assented, disappearing around the side of the hut.

Bowen lowered his spyglass, confident the ships carried the officer and skilled craftsmen he required to fix the endless problems encountered since setting sail a little over one month ago. Only briefly did he entertain the possibility of King not conceding to his requests, such was Bowen's faith in the governor. Watching the ships' progression up the river dispelled any remaining doubts. He reasoned that because King was the one who'd established the settlement on Norfolk Island, he would have an appreciation of the many difficulties now confronting them in Van Diemen's Land. Without the support of such a man, Bowen could only see disaster for the colony in the long term, its people facing mayhem and starvation.

To Bowen's delight, the *Dart* carried a subaltern officer, fourteen non-commissioned officers and privates, as well as forty-two convicts. Among the convicts, King had attempted to include the required craftsmen, there being two more stonemasons, who could be put immediately to good use in the construction of buildings.

Inside his hut, Bowen was handed a letter from Governor King by the subaltern officer, Lieutenant William Moore, which gave praise for the location and progress of the settlement at Risdon and at last confirmed his position as governor of Van Diemen's Land, but as he continued to read Bowen paled. King's instructions were succinct. The soldiers of the New South Wales Corps, now comprising twenty-two non-commissioned officers and privates, were henceforth to be under the immediate control of their new commanding officer, Lieutenant Moore. The letter stated somewhat tersely that Bowen was not to interfere with the corps or attempt to employ its men in any activity other than their military duty. Bowen read the paragraph a second time, then a third.

He had effectively been shackled.

"I trust Governor King has made my position perfectly clear," Lieutenant Moore stated. He stood to attention, facing Bowen across the table, his cap firmly tucked under his left arm. "The soldiers of the corps will be under my direct control, any communication up or down the line being directed through myself, as their commanding officer."

Bowen's cheeks stung with rage. How could King expect him to maintain control of the settlement when the soldiers were excluded from his direction? It was inconceivable. Had King taken leave of his senses? Quickly he scanned the relevant paragraph a fourth time. It read no differently; Lieutenant Moore had complete control of the corps.

"Quite clear, Lieutenant," he echoed in the same flat tone, trying to conceal the fury that all but urged him to knock the arrogance from the disposition of the man standing before him. "However, I trust you will be always open to my suggestions."

"Certainly, sir, depending on the validity of the suggestion."

Bowen's heart sickened at the sneer flickering across Moore's face, but knew it was pointless to pursue or even acknowledge the man's attitude. "There must be cooperation between us, Lieutenant," he said. "It will not do to have the men think there is a division within command. I have been appointed governor of all Van Diemen's Land, as I'm sure you're aware. My requests are to be obeyed. Is that clear?"

"Quite clear, sir, but, might I say, like it or not, there is a division in the command. Your word won't be questioned in matters not relating to the corps, sir, but it is my duty to ensure my soldiers are employed only in military pursuits. Requests for them to perform other assignments must, and will, be denied. I am informed there are convicts enough to do manual labour."

Bowen glared at Moore, who was obviously well briefed by King but still lacked any meaningful insight into the settlement's immediate difficulties advanced by the unfavourable disposition of the prisoners. The man's approach would have to change if he was to be of any use.

"Their numbers may be sufficient, but they lack the necessary skill and motivation to meet the needs of a new colony. A little assistance from the corps would not go astray. May I count on your support in that quarter, Lieutenant?"

"The corps will seek to be cooperative, sir. I can promise nothing more." His dour tone offered very little promise.

"Thank you, Lieutenant, that will be all."

Lieutenant Moore retired from the hut, an exaggerated spring in his step, leaving the disillusioned Bowen pondering the best means of dealing with this latest hurdle. Moore was some years older, had King's support, and was obviously a force to be reckoned with, but Bowen remained hopeful the man's bumptious attitude was not indicative of their future interaction.

Chapter 13

Unaware of the developments in camp, it was with heavy feet and a head aching from lack of sleep that Nicholas trudged through the bush with a hunting party led by the burly Walter Burton, who'd insisted on bringing his wife along.

Although the days were warm, last night the temperature plummeted, and along with most of the soldiers in the barracks, he awoke several times, shivering. All slept fitfully, but it was useless to complain because there were no extra blankets to be had. Instead they looked forward to warmer nights with the arrival of spring. Most of the soldiers had by now adjusted to the southern hemisphere's reversal of the seasons, but not so Nicholas, who still thought it odd to have Christmas at the height of summer when everyone would be sweltering instead of huddled around log fires as they did back in England.

"I doubt I'll ever get used to a summer Christmas," Nicholas commented.

"Oh, but you will," enthused Charlotte Burton. "If you have

the Christmas spirit, it can be just as nice, for all its differences, and it's only about nine weeks away, so we should start making our preparations now if it's to be a fine celebration."

"There'll be time enough for that, woman," grumbled her husband. "Let's concentrate on filling the stores to meet our immediate needs first."

Charlotte's exuberance was quelled by her husband's impatient practicality, and it seemed to Nicholas the pair was rather mismatched, he being older and pragmatic while she was full of youthful, almost reckless, enthusiasm. Burton, Nicholas knew, was a free settler from England with a mind of his own, as brusque as he was burly. No one ever mentioned Charlotte's background or where they were married, but despite their blatant differences, they had stayed together and already produced two children, although Charlotte hardly looked old enough.

She was not a beautiful woman by traditional standards. Instead she exuded an aura of glowing, youthful zest that captivated most of those with whom she came in contact, and Nicholas was no exception. His eyes were continually drawn to her. In a way, she reminded him of Emmeline, not so much her looks, but she possessed a similar enthusiasm for life, almost a passion, for whatever drew her attention. It surprised him that he had not thought much about Emmeline over the last few weeks and dismissed it as a good thing. She was part of the past, as was her husband, and there were more pressing things to occupy his thoughts these days.

Again his eyes went to Charlotte.

The group had travelled north for some hours without sighting game. Burton becoming irritated and disagreeable.

Although a large, white bird had been sighted earlier, it took to the air with a screech as Burton readied his weapon, leaving the shot whistling through space. The bird circled once in curiosity then flew off above the trees, squawking its triumph.

In an attempt at stealth, they proceeded to move through the dense bush as slowly and silently as possible, yet still they saw no game. By the time the sun was high, they were tired and extremely disheartened and stopped to rest in the shade of the eucalyptus trees. The day was far from hot, but their throats were dry, and all swigged heartily from water flagons as they pondered their pitiful lack of success. According to Burton, who had successfully led several earlier hunts, there should be no need to go deep into the bush because the animals came naturally to the stream for water. The idea seemed quite logical, but for all this knowledge, they had still caught nothing to put on the table.

"Perhaps they only came down at night," suggested Private David Long, Nicholas' colleague. It was the first time either of them had accompanied Burton on one of his hunting excursions.

"True," Burton replied. "Most of these animals are nocturnal, and I've certainly had more success catching kangaroos in the evenings, but once it gets dark, it's too damned hard to spot them . . . unless there's a good moon of course, and even then your aim has to be bloody good."

Seated in the small clearing shaded by the trees, the four of them discussed possible ways of improving their daytime hunting technique. Charlotte, much to Nicholas' surprise, was keen to contribute and suggested the laying of traps as a possible solution.

"This is something about which you know nothing," Burton shot at her. "I suggest you leave such things to others."

"But you wanted me to learn to hunt. That's the reason you insisted I come along."

Burton sighed at her indignant tone. "Quite so, Charlotte," he said, softening his manner. "But I was expecting you to learn first by observation. Later, when you've seen how it's done, you may put what you've learned into practice. Right now, I'd rather my wife not display her ignorance by making foolish suggestions."

Charlotte glared at her husband, a mutinous blaze in her eyes, but she said nothing and eventually lowered her gaze, shoulders slumping as she did so.

"But, why not try trapping?" questioned David Long. "It sounds like a perfectly reasonable suggestion."

"And what would you know?" Burton sneered, resenting outside support of his wife. "These animals are mostly herbivorous. You're not likely to lure any of them into a trap when their food grows everywhere. Besides, are you an expert in setting traps?"

The three exchanged quick, frustrated glances while Burton replaced the cap on his canteen and started to rise. "I thought not," he said.

Charlotte sprang to her feet. "Well, let's be off," she said brightly, her recent chastising put aside. "We can't go back empty-handed, and it can only get better from here on."

Nicholas grinned at her resilience. She needed to be an optimist, given she had to contend with such an oppressive husband. And she was right. They'd caught nothing all morning, and things couldn't get much worse, so they might as well press on and see what the afternoon would bring. But why Burton wanted his wife to be a hunter escaped him. Certainly she was healthy, strong, and resourceful enough, but there was an element of feminine fragility about her, a certain vulnerability—definitely not the quality of a hunter.

After another unsuccessful hour, Burton again called a halt. "Unless we start heading back, we won't reach the settlement by nightfall," he said. "There'll be no moon tonight, so we'd best get a move on lest we lose our way in the dark. And the blacks will be about, to be sure."

"I've seen no signs," Nicholas ventured, glancing around. "What makes you think they're around?"

"That's just it, my boy. You don't see them unless they want to be seen, but you can bet they've been watching us."

"If that's the case, then they've probably taken any game to be had in this area."

"More than likely they've intentionally scared it off so we'll all starve to death or go back to where we came from. I suspect they don't care too much for the likes of us, arriving out of nowhere and squatting on their land, no questions asked."

"I reckon they could drive us off if they had a mind to," Nicholas responded. "They must outnumber us at least ten to one."

"One hundred to one, more likely. Come on, let's get moving."

"What I mean is, they could have picked us off at any time today if they'd wanted to," Nicholas defended, refusing to believe the aborigines meant them any harm. "Surely there's enough food for all of us."

"Well, if that's so," Burton scoffed, "how is it that we've nothing to show for today's hunt? Get your head out of the clouds, boy. They don't want us here, and they'll show us exactly that soon enough."

"Burton's right, Nick," David interjected. "The blacks don't need much of an excuse to attack. You must have heard how they attacked those settlers up in the Hawkesbury region north of Sydney Town, slaughtering them without warning. I think we'd best be on our way."

Disappointed in the day, they began the return journey with Charlotte, now anxious to regain the security of the settlement, taking the lead with Nicholas. Instead of searching for game, they now scanned the bush for natives, soon forgetting they were returning empty-handed and it would be salted pork for dinner yet again.

Nicholas' thoughts returned to the stories told with such great delight by Ben Rogers about the massacre of the Durak aborigines and how the corps had planned the surprise attack, giving them no chance of survival, not even the women and children. How the corps and the settlers could justify such drastic measures was beyond his comprehension. Surely such a situation could be avoided in Van Diemen's Land because these natives exhibited no sign of hostility and kept to themselves.

A sudden scuttling in the nearby scrub brought them all to a halt, then a bellowing Walter Burton, closely followed by David Long, tore past Nicholas and Charlotte, trampling the bush in pursuit of the animal. Seconds later, there was a sickening thud followed by an agonised screech from the impaled creature.

A horrified Charlotte stood transfixed, her face drained of colour. Nicholas picked up her bayonet from where it landed after she dropped it and handed it back to her. The action brought her back to the present, and they both turned to stare down at the furry, black animal Burton tossed cheerfully at their feet. "What the devil is that?" Nicholas blurted. "It's the ugliest thing I've ever seen."

Burton put his foot on the animal's flank and withdrew his weapon. "I reckon it's one of those things that scream out in the night like they're always fighting," he said.

They'd all heard the strange sounds, ranging from growling, snorting, screeching, and even hissing, from the very first night they spent in Van Diemen's Land. Initially they were fearful some giant creature was about to attack them, but when the noise continued and nothing more eventuated, they all became used to the nighttime squabbles of the native fauna and thought little more of it.

"It looks too small to make that racket," Nicholas commented. "But it's certainly hideous enough."

"It's revolting," Charlotte whispered. "This whole thing is so horrible."

Burton surveyed his wife, whose face was still distorted with horror. "Come on, woman," he grumbled. "At least some of us will eat fresh meat tonight. It mightn't be much, but it will make a good stew."

Charlotte's bayonet fell to the ground again, coming to rest beside a rotting log as she sprinted from view. Burton followed at the sound of dry retching and found his trembling wife crouched in the undergrowth not far away, tears coursing down her pale cheeks. "I'll never be able to do what you just did," she gasped, between the involuntary spasms of her stomach. "It's revolting and . . . just so cruel. I won't come with you again, Walt. You've no right to insist that I do."

"You can do it, my dear. It'll just take a little time." He slipped a comforting arm across Charlotte's shoulders as her body heaved again. "The more you do it the easier it becomes, and you agreed I'll need your assistance if we're to make a go of it here. It has to be a combined effort until we're established. If

I'm called away for any length of time, how would you manage without some basic hunting skills? What would the children eat? I know it's hard at first, but you knew that when you agreed to come here. You'll do better next time. Just don't give up now. It's so unlike you."

Nicholas listened in silence and understood Burton's logic. The family would not prosper in Van Diemen's Land unless both pulled their weight in everything, especially their efforts to put food on the table. He had seen women forced into such an existence in the remote areas around Sydney Town, and a woman's lot in Van Diemen's Land would be little different. It was a hard life, being a pioneer, too hard for many women and even some men. They either succumbed to the continual battle for survival or found some easier existence, often freeloading, but Nicholas sensed Charlotte was different. She possessed a feminine vigour or resourcefulness—he was not sure which—and would be able to cope with many hardships. But to his mind, things like hunting should never be a woman's job. It would be far more logical for her to remain at the settlement with the two children, tending the house and garden, but Walter Burton had other ideas for his young wife, much to Nicholas' lament. He was convinced that if the lovely Charlotte had been his own wife, he would have done everything humanly possible to protect her from such hardship and brutality.

"Women," scoffed Long. "They're only good for one thing, eh, Nick? He'd do better to leave her at home to keep his bed warm."

"She'd be better off around the house," he agreed, choosing not to return Long's knowing wink. In his eyes, Charlotte Burton was above his mockery.

The Burtons rejoined them, and the four continued on their

way, enduring a recitation from Burton about how women must strive to be strong and capable, overcoming their natural weaknesses in the face of adversity for the good of their family and home. His narration was accepted silently by his wife who, still pale faced, followed him with her head down while the two soldiers plodded on behind, both preferring to remain distant and not add comment to Burton's theories.

The man was quite definite in his assertions, and his ideas sounded good in principle, but Nicholas was of the opinion few women wanted, or were even suited to, such a life and when he expressed these doubts, a spluttering, red-faced Burton turned on him. "What would you know about providing for a family?" he snarled. "I'll thank you to stay out of business that doesn't concern you. This is between me and my wife, no one else." Clearly he did not appreciate being told his wife was too admirable and gentle to be subjected to the wilds of Van Diemen's Land or the whims of an enterprising husband. "And I remind you," he continued, "Charlotte is my wife. Don't think your lovelorn looks have gone unnoticed. Keep away from her if you value your hide."

"Walter, it's not—" Charlotte began, placing her hand on her husband's arm.

"Don't interrupt," he retorted, flinging her hand away. "I intend to have my say." He turned to Nicholas. "Like I said, keep your nose out of places it doesn't belong and take your puppy love elsewhere. You've been warned. I'll not tolerate any shenanigans. Cross me, and you'll rue the day you ever laid eyes on her."

Stunned by the vehement response, Nicholas gaped, then stammered, "You've got it all wro—"

"Enough," Burton said, his arm waving a dismissal. "I'll hear no more on the subject. You can't deny what I've seen with my own eyes. Just maintain your decency and I'll be prepared to forget what's happened here today, but step out of line just once and you'll live to regret it." Firmly, he took his wife's elbow and turned toward the settlement, oblivious to the bewildered, although tender, glance Charlotte threw over her shoulder.

A mischievous backhand from a sniggering David Long caught Nicholas on the arm, and he responded with a shrug and a grin that he hoped would conceal the turmoil he felt. The last thing he wanted was for Long to think less of him by revealing it was never his intention to cause trouble between the Burtons. Certainly he had tried to hide his attraction to Charlotte, apparently without success. Now he had an enemy and unconsciously his pace slowed, allowing the Burtons a little distance.

Chapter 14

No one spoke for several miles. Even Long decided it was not his place to voice an opinion. As time passed and the familiar stream was sighted up ahead, Charlotte started feeling better about the day's events, and her spirit began to lift again. Hunger and exhaustion, it seemed, could justify almost anything, and in this case, a fresh stew would be a great improvement on the salted pork and biscuit they had endured for too long. At least the meagre success of today's hunt would tide them over until there was a more successful hunt another day.

They reached the stream some distance from camp and greedily quenched their thirsts, refilling their flagons before resting their weary bodies on the tranquil banks still warmed by the late afternoon sun. Nicholas found a log by the water and sat with his feet dangling into its biting chill, his well-worn boots, holes in their soles, at his side. Despite their shoddy state, supply of a new pair was still months away, so he resorted to reinforcing them with whatever he could get. Leather was the best, but because it was scarce, he used scraps of folded fabric torn from the bottom of shirts, and even layers of leaves and bark. In this, he was not alone, most of the troop being similarly shod.

When the trees obscured the sinking western sun, leaving them in the shade with the temperature rapidly falling, the Burtons and Long made ready to move off, but Nicholas decided to stay behind. It was still light, and with the settlement only a few hills away, no one objected. He even sensed the Burtons were as pleased to be rid of him as he was to see them go.

Once alone, a silent tranquillity, disturbed only by the gentle rustle of leaves swaying in the breeze overhead, enveloped Nicholas. A group of waterfowl flew in and landed further downstream where the water was deeper, their transition between air and water made with ease and in total silence. He wished he could be so adaptable. Convicts make their transition from England to this great southland with anxiety and regret. That was understandable, but it should be different for those who left of their own free will. Somehow he had to find a way of turning things around, especially this new thing with the Burtons.

Nicholas withdrew his feet from the water and spread his legs along the log, the cold making his skin prickle, but he was reluctant to leave. It was such a peaceful spot, he soon became absorbed in the silence, free of his worries. When the sky became tinged with red, he knew it was time to leave, but instead he closed his eyes and rested his head on bent knees, thankful for quiet respite.

A sudden splash to his right made him jump. There was nothing to see save a few distant ripples. When he heard it again, he ignored it, but the third time piqued his curiosity.

Still there was nothing to be seen. Perhaps it was fish or a bird at play.

But a tingle of fear shot up his spine as the splashing became as regular as footsteps. Someone or something was approaching through the upstream shallows. His throat tightened and his blood turned to ice when, through the dim light, emerged the form of two black-skinned men crossing the shallow stream at a long diagonal. Between them, strung on a pole, was a kangaroo, the result of a recent kill. At first they were unaware of his presence, but as soon as he made a move to get up, the two hunters stopped short, their eyes meeting Nicholas' in mutual astonishment.

All three stood momentarily paralysed, but the instant Nicholas spotted the assortment of spears and clubs in their hands, he remembered Burton's assertion of how these people resented the newcomers, and quickly regained the use of his limbs and didn't linger to determine their intentions. Half expecting a spear in the back, he fled from the creek, up along its bank, as fast as his legs and the terrain would allow, stopping for nothing, despite low branches and thick scrub clawing at his clothes. Only as a child had he been so athletic: hurdling rocks, fallen logs and bushes without a second thought, concentrating only on putting as much distance as possible between himself and the hunters.

Out of breath and exhausted, Nicholas was finally forced to a halt. From behind a tree, almost not daring to breathe, he peered back through the scrub. To his relief he saw no one, just a deserted expanse of grass, scrub, and tall trees. With the light rapidly fading, it was difficult to see clearly, but if they had given chase, somehow he had managed to lose them. Only with that knowledge did he fully succumb to his air hunger and fall back against the tree, gasping noisily. It was not until dense darkness enveloped the bush that he was capable of making his way over the hill and back to the settlement.

Chapter 15

Once in the safety of the barracks and having regained his breath and composure, Nicholas construed the aborigines were probably as equally stunned and frightened by the encounter as he had been and more than likely made no attempt at pursuit. In retrospect, they had more than enough time to hurl a spear into his back, but chose not to. Certainly, he had given them no reason to attack. Ashamed of his cowardly reaction, he chose to say nothing of the incident to David Long and the others who noisily entered the hut, anxious to convey news of the two ships' arrival.

"Now we have reinforcements, we won't have to do extra guard duty or do all that building and garden work Bowen wants," stated Long, spreading himself across the bunk opposite Nicholas. "I've heard our new commanding officer, Lieutenant Moore, is a strong fellow not about to be pushed around. There'll be no more putting up huts or digging gardens for us—probably no hunting either."

"And none too soon," Private Carr said, from the other side of the hut. "We've taken far too much abuse at Bowen's hands, and I, for one, didn't join the corps to play gardener."

"Nor I," agreed Nicholas. "But at the time, there weren't enough hands to do everything, so the duties seemed reasonable under the circumstances. I never thought it would last forever."

"If you ask me, one month of this sort of work is more than enough," interjected Private Prickett, who sat gloomily on his bunk next to Carr's. "I never asked to be sent here, and I'm damned if I'll take any more of it."

"Well, you won't have to if Moore's half the man they say he is," Long replied.

"Just as well, because the two of us are fed up with it," Carr said, speaking for Prickett as well. "And if lack of manpower isn't enough, we can't even be supplied with enough bedding to keep warm at night."

The two of them had not stopped grumbling about the extra guard duty and additional civilian duties assigned to the corps since their landing in Van Diemen's Land, but it was the first time they'd complained about provisions. While Nicholas could see their point, there had been no alternative other than complying with Bowen's requests, at least until reinforcements arrived. Now that they had their extra workforce, albeit more convicts, things should improve.

"With a man like Lieutenant Moore here, it won't make a scrap of difference to us that Bowen has been made governor of Van Diemen's Land," Long continued. "It'll soon be just like New South Wales with the corps in control of almost everything, except we're here right from the start to get in early. In a few years, we'll all be on easy street."

"Damned right," confirmed Prickett. "If we play our cards right, we'll end up as rich as John Macarthur or Henry Best. They were once in the corps."

Both men had been corps officers in Sydney Town's early

days, obtaining several large land grants and profiting greatly from the rum trade. Henry Best in particular had made enormous profits through the spirit trade and now owned a ship that kept the colony in regular supply of alcohol.

John Macarthur had made his fortune similarly. Once a lieutenant, he soon became paymaster and inspector of public works with considerable control over the colony's economy. Becoming one of the largest landholders in New South Wales, his business dealings often brought him in conflict with the early governors, but he retained his influence and developed a lucrative wool-producing enterprise.

"I can just picture myself as well off as Macarthur," mused Carr. "Hundreds of acres of land, access to free convict labour and a steady income from plying rum on the side. A man can really go places."

"First we need to find out what this place is best suited for: farming or grazing," put in Long. "That's the key. Then we can apply for land grants in the best areas, get free labour to work the land to its full potential and we're on the high street: rich in no time."

"Farming's not for me," stated Prickett. "Working the rum trade's easier."

Nicholas listened in silence. Again the corps was quick with its schemes to seize any wealth and power on offer. Nothing had changed . . . and why should it? It was inevitable Van Diemen's Land would go the same way as New South Wales. Just like the leopard and his spots, the corps cannot change its disposition. Why had he been so blind? But somehow he was unable to blame a man for wanting to better his lot.

He sighed and rolled to face the wall, turning his thoughts to Charlotte Burton.

Chapter 16

The mid-November weather was pleasantly warm as Nicholas returned from his customary early morning stroll that took him in a loop around the settlers' land and returned along the creek, his sole purpose to catch a glimpse of Charlotte Burton. Once aware of this activity, Charlotte took to slipping away from her mundane tasks, usually the washing at that hour, to steal a quick conversation. At first she merely wanted to apologise for her husband's behaviour on the hunt, but found she was attracted to the handsome, blond soldier so different to her husband and, despite misgivings and frequent bouts of guilt, she continued the meetings.

Nicholas was driven by an entirely new emotion that swamped all reason and was powerless to remain in his bunk or alter his route when the hour he might see Charlotte approached. Being with her became his sole focus, each possibility justifying his existence and dousing the importance of all other pastime, be it duty or leisure. Neither did it trouble him that Burton's accusations had now assumed the truth.

He hastened down the steep slope, his boots slipping on the

still damp, knee-high grass. Familiarity with the route meant he could now traverse it quickly without fear of falling or being seen until he was well clear of Burton land. But this morning, there was an extra spring in his step. Today was the first time they had exchanged more than words, and a smile crossed his face at the memory of her embrace and remained there until he reached the creek and tramped on toward its junction with the Derwent. As the need for silence diminished, he allowed twigs to snap under foot and absently returned the guard's wave as he passed the convict barracks. He was too absorbed in the scent of Charlotte's hair to really notice the governor's boat missing from its usual place at the landing. Assuming Bowen was off on one of his exploratory ventures, he thought little of it, but once he noticed the governor moving about near his hut higher up the hill, he knew something was wrong. He dashed back up the crude pathway and turned off in the direction of Lieutenant Moore's hut, where he was greeted by Private John Cox, his assistant. John immediately rushed off to fetch the lieutenant.

Moore paled at the news and ordered overseer Smith to immediately assemble the convicts, whereupon seven prisoners were found missing. Presumably they had stolen the boat, which was little more than fifteen feet long, and were now making their way up the eastern coast in search of freedom. Since they appeared to have neither compass nor food, it was unlikely they would get far, but a livid Bowen, once he was informed, would not rule out New Zealand as a possible destination.

"Despite the rough sea, it is feasible to cross the Tasman in such a craft," Bowen seethed, through clenched teeth. "But the question is not whether they can make it, rather, how did they find the opportunity to attempt such an enterprise? Can you answer me that, Lieutenant Moore?"

"They must have slipped past the guard, sir."

"How is that possible? Were there not two guards on duty?"

"There are always two soldiers on duty at night, as you requested, sir," Moore replied. "But I must point out, I consider the convict barracks to have been sited too close to the stream. With the guard located between them and the corps barracks, it's difficult to provide security for yourself, the sleeping soldiers, the storehouse, and the convicts. In my opinion, the settlement is far too spread out, sir."

"You made no mention of this before," Bowen snapped, appalled the man had identified a security problem and not seen fit to raise the issue before this. Moore shuffled uncomfortably and returned Bowen's stare blankly, revealing a facet of his character not previously seen. "Well?" badgered Bowen. "What have you got to say?"

"If you will forgive me, sir, given your discontent over command, I thought it best to hold my tongue, especially as I've only been here a matter of weeks. I considered there was time enough to make changes later."

"Good God, man!" Bowen thundered. "While I appreciate your regard, rest assured your inaction has increased my discontent tenfold. I am a sailor not a soldier. Don't you think I would welcome any suggestion to improve Risdon's security? This is a penal settlement, and we cannot have convicts absconding at their whim. It is the first escape from this settlement and a black day for us both—seven prisoners escaping from their barracks, seizing *my* own boat, no less, and heading off for God knows where, all without any challenge from the guard. It's preposterous! The corps has failed me, which is utterly intolerable. See to it that this cannot happen again, Lieutenant."

Reticent to leave, Moore stood his ground and stated in his familiar flat tone, "sir, I am compelled to emphasise the escape was not due to any shortcoming of the corps. Had the settlement been planned with security in mind instead of aesthetics, it would not have occurred."

Bowen was fully prepared to accept his layout of the settlement may be wanting, and undoubtedly there was accountability on both sides, but it was obvious Lieutenant Moore was not about to concede any liability whatsoever on the part of the corps.

"Lieutenant," Bowen sighed, "it is apparent there is room for improvement within both the organisation of the guard and the siting of several buildings. If we work together toward overcoming these failings, our lives will be that much the better. Do you not agree?"

"The corps has not failed, as you put it, sir," Moore stated, looking down his nose. "The error was in building the convict barracks next to the stream, right where your boat was moored."

Only to himself did Bowen concede there was an element of truth in Moore's argument, but unwilling to shoulder the entire blame himself, he critically studied the contemptuous individual before him. The ramrod stance, hardened jaw, and defiant expression clearly conveyed the fact that it was futile to argue further, especially if he ever hoped to gain any cooperation from the man. Bowen turned away, clasped his hands at his back, and moved behind the desk, where he momentarily paced back and forth staring at the floor. Then he swallowed hard. "Kindly see to it that this sort of thing cannot happen again, Lieutenant," he said, repeating his request as calmly as his turmoil allowed. "And advise me of the changes as soon as possible."

Word of the disagreement between the governor and Lieutenant Moore spread quickly, and for the next week or so, no one talked of anything else. The soldiers took bets from anyone with something to wager as to who would eventually get the upper hand. The odds were ten to one in Moore's favour. The escaped convicts, and whether they eventually made it to freedom, soon became a subject of the past as Bowen and Moore vied for supremacy over the slightest incident.

When Bowen requested Nicholas assume the role of his second assistant and work alongside Mr. Little, a surprised Nicholas wondered what he had done to gain the Governor's trust but was naturally eager to assume the post. If he performed well, it could only advance his prospects by opening further opportunities. Unfortunately, Lieutenant Moore had other ideas, insisting the corps was gaunt enough without reducing its numbers further at the whim of a self-indulgent governor.

So life remained unchanged and, as disappointed as he was, Nicholas saw some merit in Moore's decision. He also foresaw escalating conflict between the two commanding officers. Never quite able to fathom why a naval officer was sent to govern a settlement of soldiers and convicts, Nicholas inwardly supported the endeavours of the young Governor Bowen, but despite liking the man, he was outwardly obliged to attest support for his direct commanding officer, William Moore.

"Bowen is a good man," Nicholas said, letting the long strands of Charlotte's light-brown hair slip from his fingers. "He means well. It's just that everyone seems to have it in for him. I'm amazed he keeps going."

"Walt says he should never have been sent here in the first place," she replied, rolling on her side to face him, her head propped by a bent elbow.

He looked into her clear, grey eyes thoughtfully. "Most would agree," he finally said, gently removing another leaf from the tangled tresses trailing down her arm. "But let's have no talk of your husband," he continued with forced mirth, drawing her closer. "It's bad enough you have to return to him. Let's not allow him to spoil this time together."

Chapter 17

By late November, little had changed. The corps remained mutinous, the convicts uncooperative, and Bowen frustrated. Another shortage of food and supplies added to Bowen's problems.

One night, Bill Little rushed to the governor's bedroom door. "Lieutenant Bowen, sir. Something's happened. You better wake up."

"Good God, man," Bowen grumbled, "don't you know what time it is?"

"Somewhere after four, sir," his assistant continued. "And I wouldn't disturb you except for it being urgent."

"Well, what is it, man?"

"The guard on the storehouse, Private Lockwood, says the stores have been robbed, and now Lieutenant Moore is requesting to see you, sir. He's waiting in the front annex."

Bowen let out a sigh, which sounded more like a groan. The news was not entirely unexpected, especially in view of the soldiers' reluctance to perform guard duty and food again being rationed until the settlement was able to provide for its own needs. "Tell the lieutenant I'll be with him shortly," he said curtly. "And bring Lockwood to me."

Little left the room while the governor shook his head in an attempt to clear it of sleep and proceeded to fumble his way into his naval uniform.

"Couldn't this have waited until a reasonable hour, Lieutenant Moore?" Bowen asked as he entered his office still buttoning his jacket.

"I thought it best to acquaint you with the facts as soon as possible," Moore replied in his irritatingly familiar flat tone.

Bowen lowered himself into the chair behind his desk. "You may proceed."

"Private Lockwood was on guard duty by the storehouse," Lieutenant Moore said. "It was the usual type of watch with nothing out of the ordinary occurring until two other privates arrived. The three men had a conversation then walked off down by the creek for a short while. When they returned, the storehouse door was open and some of the supplies missing."

"And he saw nothing, I suppose."

"That is correct, sir. But it doesn't matter because we've caught the culprits, a group of convicts led by O'Malley, and recovered most of what was stolen."

The door opened and an unwilling Private Lockwood accompanied by Bill Little entered. Lieutenant Moore, having specifically ordered Lockwood to stay away, glared first at the guilt-ridden soldier then at the governor, realising he would have to do some suave manoeuvres if the corps was not to be blamed for this one.

"So you left your post?" Bowen asked.

Lockwood glanced nervously at Lieutenant Moore for guidance.

"Private Lockwood has informed me he was absent for no longer than fifteen minutes and was always within sight of the storehouse during this time," Moore replied.

"I was addressing the private, Lieutenant Moore," Bowen shot at him, aware of the lieutenant's intent to cover up details which might reflect badly on the corps.

"I would prefer to present you with the facts myself, sir."

"I have no doubts of that, Lieutenant, but I'm sure Private Lockwood is capable of answering a few simple questions for me." Then turning to the soldier, "Is that not so, Private Lockwood?"

Visibly wilting under Moore's stare, the man replied lamely, "I'll do me best, sir."

"Then tell me in your own words what happened."

"W . . . w . . . well, s . . . sir," Lockwood stuttered, trying to avoid eye contact with the resentful Moore. "The w . . . w . . . watch was all qu . . . qu . . . quiet as usual, with nearly everyone asleep an' all, when two of me mates came along for a chat an' the like. You know how it is, sir?" Bowen remained unmoved, so the man continued. "Well, we went for a stroll down by the creek, for no more 'n ten or fifteen minutes, I swear, but when we came back the stores was pilfered."

"And how did the thieves gain access to the stores?" asked Bowen.

"With the key, sir."

"Do you mean to tell me you left it behind when you went strolling away from your post with two other soldiers? Would you not consider that to be a major dereliction of duty, Private Lockwood?"

"Not at the time, sir. Everyone else was in bed."

"Apparently not everyone," Bowen said, his cynicism slicing the air. "And you didn't see who did the pilfering, Private?"

"No, sir, but it's turned out to be some of them convicts. Who else would do such a thing?"

"Who else indeed?" Bowen looked squarely at Moore, who remained silent, then back to Lockwood. "Tell me, Private, who were these visitors of yours who arrived for a chat in the wee small hours when everyone else was asleep?"

"I see no need to involve innocent men, sir," Lieutenant Moore interrupted. "They were merely visiting a mate executing an arduous guard duty, nothing more."

"Do you consider enticing a man from his duty to be an act of friendship, Lieutenant Moore?" the governor roared, his hand slamming down on the desk. "I suggest this was not an innocent visit, but a ploy to lure the guard away, thus providing an opportunity for the thieves."

"The notion is outrageous," Moore blustered, enraged the governor had identified the flaw in Lockwood's story and formed similar suspicions to his own unvoiced assumption. "My men would never stoop to such a lowly act. I must object in the strongest terms, sir."

"You may object all you like, Lieutenant, but it will not alter the facts that regrettably place certain members of the corps under suspicion. I demand to be told the names of the others involved."

Bowen, intent on an answer, and Moore, demanding silence, cast intimidating stares at the trembling Lockwood, who knew if he implicated his friends they would surely make him pay, yet if he remained silent, he alone would be blamed. After an uncomfortably long silence, he eventually whined, "I can't dob me mates in, sir."

"You had better come forth with their names," Bowen threatened. "Otherwise I'll have no other choice but to conclude the visit by these men was fabricated on your part to protect yourself when, in fact, it was you who collaborated with the thieves and willingly gave them entry to the storehouse."

"That's not true, sir," Samuel Lockwood wailed, his eyes pleading for assistance from his commanding officer, but Moore, concluding it was not in his interest to be seen to side with felons, offered none.

"Then give me their names, Private," Bowen demanded.

A broken Lockwood chose to endure the wrath of his colleagues rather than face a possible court martial and begrudgingly yielded. "Will Tanner an' Ed Smythe," he finally whispered, hanging his head.

"Thank you, Private," Bowen replied. "That will be all . . . for now."

When the man left the room Bowen again turned to Moore, who was flushed and sweating despite the room's early morning chill. "Tell me about Tanner and Smythe," he demanded.

"Private Edward Smythe was posted to guard your own quarters, sir, and Private William Tanner was off duty," Moore replied.

"So Tanner was probably the one sent to lure Lockwood and Smythe away while O'Malley and his cronies helped themselves to government property."

"Nothing's proven, sir," Moore objected. "Tanner doesn't seem the type."

"And just what is the type, Lieutenant?"

Moore groped for words, and Bowen savoured his discomfort, refusing to feel sorry for the man who would do all in his power to ensure the corps was not found culpable in anything. Perhaps this was a good thing as far as the corps was concerned, but Bowen's priorities demanded the matter be pursued.

"It's my understanding," Bowen continued, "Lockwood and Smythe have relatively good records aside from their continual grumbling. Tanner, on the other hand, is a known cheat, always trying to swindle a better deal for himself, particularly when it comes to food. I would not put it past him to collaborate with O'Malley if it meant putting something in his mouth."

"As I've said, sir, there's no proof, and I really have my doubts that any soldier of the corps would conspire with convicts to commit theft. It goes against what the corps stands for. I suggest the matter be dropped."

"It is too serious a matter to be swept aside, Lieutenant," Bowen said. "I suggest you thoroughly interrogate the three soldiers involved and present me with the facts after breakfast. Meanwhile I shall question O'Malley and the others. That way, we will get to the bottom of this unfortunate incident."

When they came together later in the day, Lieutenant Moore almost cheerfully informed Bowen that despite rigorous questioning, none of his soldiers had admitted any guilt and especially not to conspiring with felons. Tanner, it seemed, had merely suffered from insomnia and went out in search of company to relieve his boredom.

"Tanner is lying," Bowen stated. "O'Malley has pointed the finger at him. It was he who had the task of getting rid of the guards and ensuring the key was left behind."

"It's O'Malley's word against Tanner's," Moore defended, refusing to accept the soldier was guilty. "Who will believe the word of a convict?"

"I believe it to be true," stated Bowen. "He has no reason to lie and nothing to gain from it."

"Nothing but the satisfaction of seeing a corps man receive punishment for that which he is not guilty," Moore retorted.

"Who's to say O'Malley hasn't got it in for him for some reason?"

"You're letting sentiment and loyalty to the corps cloud your judgment."

"Private Tanner is a good soldier and not guilty of what he is accused. I will not punish him on the flimsy evidence of convicts, especially one who repeatedly offends."

"Lieutenant Moore," Bowen grimaced, his patience evaporated. "There is good evidence Tanner was in cahoots with the convicts, and he must be disciplined accordingly. I will not be drawn into any argument over the qualities, good or bad, of this man. That is my final word on the matter."

Moore's face assumed the hue of his crimson jacket. "Private Tanner will receive no disciplinary action on such scant evidence. Furthermore, I am appalled someone in your office would take the word of a felon over the sworn word of a soldier."

Again Bowen was confronted by his lack of disciplinary powers outside the navy, leaving true law and order some eight hundred miles away in Sydney Town. If Tanner were to go unpunished with Lieutenant Moore's approval, both convicts and corps would rightly believe they had free reign; chaos would soon be rife.

Unable to stomach the situation any longer, Bowen exploded in a torrent of rage. "I cannot tolerate a soldier who assists convicts to plunder the stores, much less a lieutenant who wilfully obstructs my every request. Right from the start, the soldiers here complained of the so-called hard duty of mounting one sentry by day and two by night. I erroneously thought your arrival would see a remedy of the situation, but little has improved, and supervision of the convicts is practically negligible, as the events of last night testify. And that's not to mention the escape of those seven convicts, in my own boat no less, just weeks after your arrival. Thank God they were picked up and turned in by Bass Strait sealers before Governor King got word of it. Lord knows what would have happened if they had reached New Zealand, or worse still, Timor."

Moore remained silent.

"It is my belief, Lieutenant," Bowen continued, "both the corps and the convicts regard this settlement as some sort of respite from the rigid supervision of Sydney Town. Well, I will not have it, I tell you! This is a place for secondary offenders, and discipline will be maintained. I will not stand for this division in command any longer, and I intend to appeal personally to Governor King for the immediate rectification of the problem. Private Tanner will accompany me to Sydney Town where he will undergo the appropriate military investigation that is so lacking here. That is all, sir."

Chapter 18

In late January, Bowen departed the settlement of Risdon after taking passage to Sydney Town on a whaler, the *Ferret*, that happened to enter the Derwent. True to his word, he took with him the ringleader in the store theft incident, Private Tanner, so that justice might be served.

Bowen, having had more than enough of the problems besieging Risdon, also had it in mind to resign his position as lieutenant governor and continue on with his naval career in the conflict with France. But on his arrival, Governor King was furious he had left the infant settlement without a commanding officer, and the bewildered Bowen found himself severely castigated for leaving his post.

"Furthermore," King glowered, "had you remained at your post you would have received the correspondence I dispatched last November advising you of Lieutenant Governor David Collins' expedition. He's been commissioned by the British Government to establish a settlement at Port Phillip but has since found the site unsuitable, and as an alternative, I have offered either Port Dalrymple or the Derwent." King paused, gauging Bowen's reaction and, seeing none, continued. "My guess is he will select the latter, and if that be the case, you are directed to immediately hand over the Risdon settlement to Collins along with all stores and persons currently under your command together with all documents from me with respect of your command. Is that clear?"

King's words detonated a gaping hole in Bowen's stomach, through which his entire world rushed. He was stripped of his command. Not because of anything he had done—the decision had been made months ago—but simply because of whom Collins was.

The man had entered the marines in 1770, served in America, where he fought the colonists at Bunker Hill and earned promotion to first lieutenant. After marrying and returning to England, he sailed with the First Fleet to New South Wales as Judge Advocate and later became secretary to the governor before again returning to England. Following a brief, but successful career as a writer, Collins then sought to return to the antipodes, landing himself the position of lieutenant colonel of the proposed settlement of Port Phillip. Bowen had no hope against such a man.

"I understand perfectly, sir," he said, repressing a surge of emotion and praying Collins would select Port Dalrymple on the north coast of Van Diemen's Land rather than his own Risdon.

"Then you may ready the *Integrity* to sail. You are directed to go immediately to Port Phillip in case Collins has not yet left for Van Diemen's Land, and if he has already moved on, you're to follow on to his next destination. After you've relinquished your command to Collins, you will be required here to assist in the prosecution of Private Tanner."

"Certainly, sir."

"And one more thing . . . I would expect a man in your position to act with honour. A man of character does not simply up stakes and leave a woman and her unborn child stranded."

Bowen didn't think his cheeks could feel hotter. "I have arranged for Reverend Knopwood to see to the needs of Miss Hayes, sir."

King cast a look of contempt at the man before him and snapped, "Be that as it may, I suggest you reconsider your personal responsibilities in relation to any further thoughts of altering your situation." He then put an end to the encounter with a curt, "That is all," while Bowen was still searching for words.

Deflated by having his integrity questioned and defeated in his career pursuits, Bowen turned and quietly left the office thinking how incongruous it was that he would be travelling on a ship named *Integrity*. He resisted the urge to slam the door. It would only cause more ill will, and he didn't want to add rudeness to the list of his apparent transgressions. Instead he hastened to prepare for another voyage south. Perhaps some good could yet be salvaged.

After setting sail, the *Integrity* was beset by one problem after another. When Bowen finally arrived at Port Phillip, he was informed by the few families who had chosen to remain there that the rest of the lieutenant governor's expedition, some two hundred and sixty people, had already departed for the Derwent.

Bowen immediately set off for Van Diemen's Land in a ship with a damaged rudder, sick at heart that the events of the preceding months had turned into a farce and destiny had deigned him a portrait of ridicule.

In mid-February 1804, only five months after the arrival of Bowen's party in Van Diemen's Land, Lieutenant Governor David Collins was in his forty-seventh year and not lacking in experience. His contingent of two ships, the *Ocean* and the *Lady Nelson*, sailed into the Derwent and established the settlement of Hobart at Sullivan's Cove on the far side of the river, approximately five miles downstream from Risdon. The site had the magnificent Mount Wellington, not dissimilar to Cape Town's Table Mountain, as its backdrop and a small stream flowing into the cove.

The vessels were unloaded by boat at Hunter's Island, a site providing natural security for the stores, while the main settlement was commenced a short distance away on the western shore of the Derwent. Tents were soon pitched and convicts set to work clearing the surrounding land of tall gum trees and dense, tea-tree scrub to allow the lieutenant governor's tent to be erected on a gentle slope overlooking the cove with Reverend Knopwood next door and other officers nearby.

Chapter 19

The new activity on the river attracted the curiosity of the Risdon settlement, and a small group of men soon set out to pay the newcomers a visit.

Nicholas admired the new site as the soldiers' long boat pulled into the cove. There was an abundance of low-sloping land suitable for settlement and cultivation, which was not available at Risdon, and although convict labour had not yet finished clearing the foreshore area, he judged there were several square miles of arable land beyond the trees before rolling hills swept up toward Mount Wellington. It was a magnificent sight indeed, as was the bay, which was deep enough to give safe anchorage and contained a small, tree-covered island that could be reached by foot only at low tide. The commanding officer, Nicholas concluded, was very cunning in utilising the feature for securing the settlement's stores.

Collins received the group with no more than the usual courtesy and, given Bowen remained absent, expressed concern at their leaving Risdon under minimal guard to pay him a visit, but after giving Lieutenant Moore a brief outline of his plans for the new settlement, he allowed the party to wander freely, provided they return to Risdon before nightfall.

The men strolled through the clatter of a myriad of convict activities. Most were sawing logs the tree fellers had brought in, while others split them into long slabs ready for the building construction team. Still others were making nails, sewing canvas, or carting stores and equipment back and forth. Everyone had a job to do, and all under the watchful eyes of the guards.

Off to one side, several female convicts were tilling a newly turned garden, and because of his farming interest, Nicholas left the group and wandered over. "What crop will you be sowing here?" Nicholas inquired of the woman closest to him, vigorously swinging a hoe. She was older than the rest and appeared to be directing them.

"Not been told nothin' yet," the woman snapped, not lifting her head. "Our job's to prepare the soil, not ask questions. Dare say we'll find out soon enough."

"You're from Scotland?" he asked, recognising the lilt in her voice.

"Don't make no difference now," she said flatly. "What would it be to you anyway?"

They're all the same, Nicholas thought. Too damn sullen to answer a simple question, especially if it's asked by someone in uniform. "Just making conversation." He turned back in search of the overseer.

It was then he saw her: a younger, darker, and more exotic version of Emmeline Thornridge, laden with newly hewn plant stakes, walking toward him. Even under such a load her movements were graceful, her smile free and her expression serene, at least until she became aware of his stare, whereby she lowered her eyes and hurried past, dropping her load with a pile of other stakes at the edge of the garden.

"That's the last of them for now," she said, wiping her forearms of any residue.

Her skin was still smooth and clear, something that quickly evaporated under the sun of the antipodes. "What's this, another Scot?" Nicholas ventured, succumbing to the desire to engage her in conversation, despite a fear the constriction in his throat would betray his ardour and she think him foolish. "And what parts would you be from, ma'am?"

She turned slowly, meeting his gaze. "It's Miss," she said, with a suspicious half smile that belied her amusement at being addressed so formally by a soldier. "And I'm from the Highlands. Argyll to be precise."

"Best get back to work, Maggie," the older woman ordered.

"A Highland Lassie called Maggie," he smiled, ignoring the interruption, intent on savouring the sight standing proudly, almost defiantly, before him. *Statuesque* was the word that sprung to Nicholas' mind.

"The name's Margaret McKinnon, but most folks just call me Maggie."

"You'll have bloody Gleeson on our backs again if you're not careful," the woman hissed, hacking angrily at the ground. "Get back to work."

Assuming Gleeson was the overseer, she was right . . . for over Maggie's shoulder Nicholas saw him striding toward them. So, quickly taking his leave of the women, he rounded the garden and intercepted the man about thirty yards off.

"I was enquiring as to the progress of the garden," Nicholas said, taking the man's elbow and steering him away toward the trees. "They're making excellent inroads. Tell me, how do you get such cooperation?"

Gleeson shrugged an acknowledgment and glanced over his shoulder, ensuring the women were back at work before freeing his arm and following, drawn by a new face and the prospect of stimulating conversation. "You can't give an inch," he said eagerly, "because as soon as they spot a weakness, you're a target." Nicholas nodded his understanding as they wandered over to the edge of the clearing and made themselves comfortable in the shade of a tall gum tree, where they sat for half an hour while an unwitting Gleeson continued to espouse the intricacies of convict discipline. But Nicholas' eyes followed Maggie McKinnon's every move.

The women kept a close eye on the pair under the tree. Maggie's eyes in particular were drawn to the newcomer.

"It won't do you any good flirting with the likes of him, Maggie McKinnon," the older woman warned. "It'll come to nought. He's from the Camp, you know?"

"Yes, but he's different, and I've not been called *ma'am* in a while. Besides, what's the harm in talking? Don't tell me you think he isn't handsome."

"Well, I don't," she snapped. "And the harm is you getting us all on half rations, or worse, for your silly time-wasting."

"Oh, Eadie," Maggie laughed. "I wasn't flirting, and anyone would think we were talking for an hour instead of a few minutes."

"That's how it starts," Eadie said flatly, chopping down hard with the hoe.

Nicholas tossed from side to side, his bunk groaning in the darkness, as thoughts of Maggie swirled through his slumber and dragged him, sweating, to consciousness. All thoughts of Charlotte Burton were eclipsed by visions of Maggie's azure eyes and lustrous ebony hair, through which he longed to run his fingers. Being a soldier, he could easily take her if he wanted. The military would turn a blind eye if he forced himself on her—it happened all the time—but he saw Maggie as beyond such impropriety and he, himself, wanted more. Yet common sense told him there could never be anything more because it was entirely unacceptable for a free man to take a convict to wife. Convicts married convicts. That was the way it was and always would be. They were, after all, the lowest in the social hierarchy, except perhaps for the aborigines, who did not rate at all.

But there was no room for logic in his passion, and it played no part in his decision to return to Collins' settlement as soon as the opportunity presented. Somehow he was going to have Maggie McMcKinnon. He would make it happen. Of that he was sure.

Chapter 20

The *Integrity* encountered further difficulties off Cape Barren Island, inducing an exasperated Bowen to charter a schooner they encountered to convey him back to the Derwent. He arrived in March and was immediately informed by Lieutenant Moore that Collins had found the Risdon site unsuitable for his settlement.

"He admitted this was a better site than Port Phillip," Moore continued, "but he still found it wanting and not worth expanding, so moved his people five miles downriver to Sullivan's Cove."

"Yes, yes, Lieutenant. Having seen the encampment as I came in, I gathered as much," Bowen said dismissively. "I'll visit Lieutenant-Governor Collins tomorrow."

"Collins has called his settlement *Hobart*, sir." Moore's gloating was barely concealed, and Bowen's mood sank to a level he had not thought possible, for this was the name he had planned for the Risdon site. During his many hours at sea, Bowen had given much thought to his situation. It was undoubtedly the beginning of the end. Collins was here to take over Van Diemen's Land and push him out, of that there was no doubt, but he was not about to go without a fight.

The next day, a light mist hung over the water as Bowen's small party pushed off from the Risdon shore, heading downstream toward Hobart with Nicholas, one of the first to volunteer for oar duty, putting his growing skill and strength into each stroke. The farthest thing from his mind was today's abandoned rendezvous with Charlotte, for he was off to see Maggie again.

Resolved in his intention not to relinquish his command just because Port Phillip had proved unworthy, Bowen mentally rehearsed over and over what he would say to Collins when they arrived. In his opinion, Collins should have taken his party to Port Dalrymple on the Tamar River in the north of Van Diemen's Land and, in doing so, halt any remaining French interest in the island, thus securing it for England. Surely it was not too late to convince him of the idea's merit.

But all his rehearsing came to nothing when Collins came straight to the point. "The Tamar is close to New South Wales and will be settled soon enough," he said. "It's the southeast part of the island that remains at risk. The French won't bother with the southwest coast—it's far too rugged to be of any interest—so we must consolidate our position on the Derwent. That's why I'm here. As far as I am concerned, you may remain at Risdon, but I expect to be informed of the camp's activities and consulted in all major decisions. Is that clear?"

"Certainly," Bowen said, realising he had not been completely stripped of his command as expected. Perhaps the two of them could develop a mutually agreeable alliance over time. For the first time in weeks, Bowen felt more positive about the situation.

But one thing still really galled him.

Risdon had been dubbed *The Camp* by the Hobart settlement, an insult that vexed him to the core. Although the settlement contained less than one hundred people, it should, in Bowen's opinion, be accorded the respect due a first settlement, but not wishing to incur the lieutenant governor's wrath, he kept his silence. The man had been honest and courteous, spending more time with him than his busy schedule should allow, so after refreshments, Bowen took his leave for a guided tour of the rapidly developing settlement.

In the meantime, Nicholas found Maggie working on another garden situated in an area that had been uncleared on his previous visit. She noticed him immediately, stood upright, and wiped the dust from her face with an equally dusty apron before greeting him with one of her captivating, broad smiles.

"Back so soon, Private Thomas?" she said, returning to her task.

"Aha!" he said, with satisfaction. "So you've asked about me?" His grin was that of a man who understands that what he wants might be there for the taking.

"It's easy enough to find out a name."

"But you were interested enough to remember it, weren't you?"

"Well don't go hanging your hat on it, Private," she laughed. "Things aren't always as they seem. Besides, Gleeson was only too eager to talk about you and the Camp after you'd gone. Not in a nasty way, mind, but he can be a right chatterbox when you get him going."

"I noticed," he said, amusement in his eyes. "So what have you concluded?"

She raised her head and squinted into the morning sun. "About what?"

"Me."

"Well, now, let's see," she discarded the hoe and wiped her hands. "If your manner is anything to go on, you're fully aware that you are very easy on the eyes, but I think perhaps you're looking for what you want in entirely the wrong places."

Even though she had seen right through him, Nicholas refused to be put off and said, "Isn't that for me to decide?"

Again serious, she grabbed the hoe. "Not if one party thinks otherwise," she said, ripping at the soft, tilled earth. "We're from different worlds with nothing in common."

"Then we shall just have to rectify that." Nicholas removed his hat and seated himself in a position commanding a good view of the new garden and its surrounds, yet close enough to allow easy conversation with her. "My mother always said there's only one way to find common ground and that's by talking, so what would you fancy chatting about on this fine, sunny morning, my Highland Lassie?

Maggie couldn't suppress a laugh. "You're far too sure of yourself, Private Thomas," she chided, nonetheless intrigued by the confident soldier who still followed his mother's advice. Perhaps it said something about the character of the man.

"That's been said of me on more than one occasion," he grinned, thinking it was really more the opposite. "And you can call me Nicholas, if you like."

Her gaze was unfathomable, but he dwelt not on what thoughts may be tumbling through her mind, for at least he had made a start in getting to know her, and hopefully it would prove to be the first of many garden-side conversations they would share. In time, perhaps she would come to enjoy them as much as he.

Chapter 21

In March, Martha Hayes gave birth to Bowen's daughter, Henrietta, in their small hut on the hill at Risdon. Of course it was warm and dry inside, Bowen had seen to that, but it was hardly what she imagined life would be like before leaving Sydney Town and definitely not what she desired for their child's entry into the world.

Martha was well aware of the settlement's problems, despite Bowen's attempts to shield her, so she didn't complain; there was little point. He had enough on his mind, and she was grateful to him for bringing her mother and stepfather back with him on the *Integrity*. She had missed her mother terribly over the past months and surmised Bowen, being aware of this, sought to both please her and have someone experienced present to assist with childbirth. Convinced of his worth and good intentions, Martha stood by her man and continued to give her support wherever possible.

Meanwhile, daily life at Risdon continued much as before

with convicts grumbling and soldiers, for the most part, pleasing themselves.

Nicholas, on the other hand, became committed to supervising the work on the government garden, seeing it as a possible stepping stone to improving his prospects. Some days, when Lieutenant Moore wasn't about, he didn't mind getting his hands dirty and would even pitch in and help with the digging. It was a crisp, sunny morning, and he was out supervising the groundbreaking in readiness for another garden bed, when he became aware of a silent figure beside him.

It was Charlotte.

"What happened?" she whispered. "I waited for ages, until it was too cold to stay longer. Is everything all right?"

He ignored her questioning gaze, took her by the elbow instead, and guided her beyond the work area and out of the hearing of prying convict ears while he groped for an explanation.

"Things have changed since Collins' party arrived." he said, gesturing down river. "I wasn't able to get away. I've been assigned extra duty, helping out down there. You know how it is."

Charlotte nodded, although she didn't know how it was. She always found time for him. She drew her shawl in closer and contemplated his words while gazing, unseeing, across the cold, silent river that was like the sudden gap between them. "Then I'll wait until I receive word from you," she said at last, lowering her smarting eyes.

"I think that's best."

He watched her walk up the hill, her pace slow, almost reluctant. Did she know he had lied? For a moment, he longed to take her in his arms. The last thing he ever wanted was to hurt her, but then his thoughts went to Maggie, and he knew, without question, it was she he was going to have. In that moment, it became easy to rationalise that the feelings he and Charlotte shared were never meant to be anyway. She was married and both had known they could only ever share a few snatched moments; it was destined to end right from the start. What never occurred to Nicholas was that he would be the one to walk away. He should have learned his lesson over Emmeline Thornridge; nothing lasting or good ever came from such dalliances.

Absently he kicked the pile of stones cleared from the garden area. Charlotte deserved better. She deserved the truth. Again Nicholas' eyes followed her trudging steps, knowing he could never bring himself to tell her. Just imagining her pain tore his stomach. He grabbed a stone and hurled it toward the river, watching it fall short and bounce down the slope. A second stone fell likewise, as did another thrown with greater force, and another, and another. Not until his arm ached did he turn away, concluding it was best to let the whole thing with Charlotte simply slide.

While the Risdon soldiers continued to do exactly as they liked without fear of repercussions, Nicholas was free to focus all his attention on Maggie, and he visited her regularly. If he was unable to secure a position in the boat used by the corps on routine trips to Hobart, he either took the craft himself or managed to persuade one of his colleagues to row him across the river, from where he would make his way downstream on foot. A signal on his return would bring the same man out to collect him. Such service came at a cost—part of his meagre rations—but it was well worth it. His relationship with Maggie thrived.

They had long conversations, during which Nicholas learned Maggie came from a tiny town on the Ardnamurchan peninsula in Argyllshire and was the eldest daughter in a family of twelve children. Times were hard, with barely enough food on the table to go around, and when their father took ill and died, the burden on the family was overwhelming. Faced with possible starvation, Maggie and her elder brother Donald stole a sheep from a neighbouring farm, and for nearly a month, they could put food in the mouths of their brothers and sisters. Lucky enough to get away with it the first time, some weeks later they tried it again, but a suspicious farmer caught them in the act, and they were tried and sentenced to death. Some of the villagers, aware of the family's plight, sent in a petition and, perhaps because of this, their sentences were commuted to transportation for life. Brother and sister had been separated since their arrest, causing them to lose contact, and Maggie now had no idea where Donald was. Tears still came to her eyes when she thought of him and her family back in Scotland left with younger brother Angus, just fourteen years old, to fend for them.

Nicholas had heard similar tales, but until now never felt any compassion, not even when it was said people were transported for stealing the likes of a loaf of bread. Stealing was stealing and should not go unpunished. Yet the pain in Maggie's eyes spoke otherwise, and he found himself giving comfort by offering improbabilities.

"Donald could well be in Sydney Town right now," he said.

"And may eventually get sent to Van Diemen's Land. Or he could be sailing here direct from Britain."

Maggie gave a wan smile and shook her head. She had long ago given up hope of ever seeing any of her family again.

"But you must never think like that," he insisted. "Without hope there's nothing."

Of course Nicholas knew Maggie had not given up hope on everything. That was one of the most endearing things about her. She was determined to make the most of her situation. Keenly aware of the prospects this fine land offered, she intended to gain her ticket-of-leave, settle down on a good piece of land and make it work for her, something Nicholas could totally identify with, but he was yet to tell her he had hopes she might wish to settle down with him.

It was late March when they were out gathering firewood way beyond Hobart's immediate surrounds that Nicholas offered to show Maggie the Risdon campsite. She readily agreed.

Along the way they gathered small piles of wood left in readiness for collection on their return journey, because questions would be asked if Maggie returned empty-handed. There were two small promontories to negotiate, but Nicholas, now familiar with the terrain, proceeded along an inland shortcut to bypass the first one. It was a strenuous hike, but both were fit, and once back at the riverbank, they advanced toward the northern tip of the second promontory from where they could see Risdon.

"It's so small," she gasped, amazed at its cramped position on a hill surrounded by more hills.

"Yes," Nicholas agreed, "but one day there will be a town here large enough to swallow the two settlements.

"You're nought but a dreamer, Nick," she laughed, taking his hand and walking to a grassy area under the trees where they still had a clear view of the river. There she sat down, indicating he should sit beside her.

"That may be right, but Sydney Town is already quite a sprawl and just think of the size of London."

"Surely you don't imagine a London here?" Her eyes danced, but she no longer laughed at him. "It's grown to what it is now over more than a thousand years."

"Yes, but what's to say it can't happen here?"

"Maybe nothing, Mr. Optimist," she laughed, rising to her feet. "Anyway, you and I won't be around to see it, and we'd better not stay here for much longer either. Time's getting away."

Nicholas grabbed her before she could step away, pulling her down to her knees. "The sun's still high. We've plenty of time."

"Some would say you're up to no good, Private Thomas." Maggie wrestled within his grasp, a throaty laugh bubbling forth at his playful attempts to confine her struggles. "Let me go, you scoundrel."

"Not a chance," he chuckled. Impishly she tried to push him away, but he simply held her tighter until finally she gave one mighty shove at the precise moment he chose to let go. She tumbled backward and lay there laughing uncontrollably, her dishevelled hair strewn across the grass.

"You're so beautiful when you're happy." There was a strange tightness in his voice as he moved closer, reached for her head of lustrous, jet-black hair, and lifted her face to his. Her lips were tense with sudden nervousness, but warm and sweet beyond belief. He kissed them over and over until they parted under the pressure of his own lips. Shivers of desire swept back and forth through their bodies. Gently he laid her back again, loosening her clothing, her slender waist and breasts smooth to his touch.

Oblivious to anything else, they clung to each other amid the tangled grass as the treetops rustled gently overhead, and he kissed her again, this time with greater urgency. Her lips were no longer tense, and she became soft and supple in his arms. Urgency turned to frenzy as their bodies sought to become one. Every fibre of his being screamed for her: the swell of her breasts, the touch of her skin, the smell of her hair. Even the taste of her mouth sent his senses soaring to a passion such as he had never known before. Nothing mattered but this moment and this woman. Their natural rhythm gained momentum, and somewhere in the core of his soul, he vowed never to be free of her arms, for she clung to him as desperately as he to her.

"I love you, Maggie," he groaned, but her reply was lost to him as he melted into her in total ecstasy then collapsed utterly spent into her arms.

Moments later they lay in silence gazing up at the gently swaying branches feeling totally complete. Somehow everything seemed clearer, colours brighter than ever before, and Nicholas gently drew her closer knowing nothing would part them now.

"I've loved you since the first moment I saw you. You know that, don't you?" he said tenderly.

Maggie raised herself to one elbow and placed a hand on his chest, her eyes soft with adoration. "Yes," she barely whispered. "I've always known; and I love you too."

Nothing more needed to be said, and smiling, he reached for her again.

Chapter 22

At Risdon, Bowen began to relax as things started to settle down and it looked like his problems might finally be over, but toward the end of April the military mutinied, refusing to mount the usual guard, and he immediately sent for Lieutenant Moore.

"This is preposterous," Bowen blustered, as a red-faced Moore entered the room. "What is your explanation, sir? I won't tolerate disobedience, as you well know."

"It's very simple, sir. The men refuse to mount the guard because it's too hard. Insufficient manpower has made the hours of duty far too long, and according to Private Carr, because of illness their constitutions are unable to bear it. The rations are hardly enough to keep up a man's strength."

Bowen considered Moore's reply. Perhaps there was some truth to it. There were six non-commissioned officers, three sergeants, and three corporals, which left only a few privates to perform guard duty. Certainly there had been sickness, nothing too serious, but it was undoubtedly compounded by the shortage of food. And that was not all. One man had been sent with Mr. Brown on a botanical excursion and another allocated to

Lieutenant Moore as his assistant. A quick calculation revealed there were only three remaining privates for guard duty, two at his own hut and one at the store.

"Their numbers may be few, it's true, but we are not yet at starvation point." Bowen said, coldly. "There will be no insubordination for whatever reason while I am in command of Risdon. Had the men pointed out their grievance, perhaps something could have been arranged with Lieutenant Governor Collins across the river that would have relieved the situation. Instead of stating that they could not mount the guard, they said they would not, and I cannot let such mutinous action go unpunished."

"The men have done their best, sir," Moore defended.

"I have my doubts about that," he glared at Moore. "Have Private Carr confined immediately."

"With all due respect, sir, that will reduce the guard further."

"That will be all, Lieutenant Moore."

Not long after this incident, a plot to seize the storehouse and escape with the provisions was discovered, whereupon an incensed Bowen, without consulting Lieutenant Governor Collins, had the storekeeper and the eight other culprits arrested. He then loaded them into his boat and set off for an island in Norfolk Bay, southeast of both settlements. There they were marooned with meagre provisions while Bowen went off in pursuit of his favourite pastime: exploration. Crossing the Derwent estuary, he proceeded up the Huon River, an endeavour that lasted almost one month.

With Bowen away, the military, naturally, did as they pleased. Nicholas took advantage of additional time with Maggie, who managed to slip away frequently now that the convicts were permitted to forage in the wooded areas far beyond the Hobart settlement due to the shortage of food. Amazingly, no one had yet tried to abscond, the perceived threat of the natives and the unknown terrain enough to keep them in check. As a result, all manner of strange creatures were brought in. Of course there were the usual kangaroos and wallabies, but mostly they could not even guess as to their names. Nobody cared, of course. So long as there was food in the pot they were satisfied. As far as the additional freedom was concerned, it was something to be enjoyed while it lasted, because ultimately it would end. Everyone knew the lieutenant governor would draw in the reigns as soon as the colony was self-sufficient. It was a prison colony after all.

Meanwhile, the situation worked to Nicholas and Maggie's advantage, she being able to meet him without anyone ever knowing he visited, and almost always he came with something for her to take back so her excursions would not appear unproductive to any onlooker. Sometimes it would be a small animal he caught or a kerchief of berries. Very rarely did she return empty-handed.

It was a clear, crisp morning in May that turned out to be one Nicholas would long remember, for on that day Maggie told him she was going to have his baby.

His voice etched with alarm. "Are you sure?"

"Of course I'm sure," she snapped, pulling free of his grasp. "And obviously you don't want it. That's quite clear from your face. Well, let me tell you it's not something I exactly planned for myself either, to be unmarried and pregnant. I don't know what to do, and I'm scared." Tears welled in her eyes.

Her vulnerability made Nicholas forget his own fear, and he reached for her. This was all Maggie needed to surmount her anguish, and she fell easily into his embrace, his left hand stroking her hair as she lowered her head to his shoulder. In his arms she was always safe. The possibility of pregnancy, although ever present, was something neither of them had bothered to dwell on, but the more Nicholas thought about it, the more he liked the idea.

"Don't worry, my darling," he whispered, her hair soft on his lips. "I'll request the lieutenant governor's permission for us to get married. Everything will be all right. Just leave it to me."

It would be a complicated matter, seeing that Collins and Bowen would both need to be involved, but he was sure permission would be granted. Dispensations were accorded men like Bowen, but the rest of them were encouraged to uphold moral decency, so to allow a child to be born out of wedlock definitely wouldn't aid the cause. As for what his colleagues thought, he couldn't care less.

Nicholas' confidence lifted Maggie's spirits and smiling, she gazed up, allowing the tears to be wiped away by his gentle fingers. All she wanted was to be with him, to have his children and live happily together.

"We will have a fine son," she said, sweeping damp strands of hair from her face. "He'll be just like his father, to be sure."

"Or a bonny wee lassie like her mother," he laughed, lifting her high and swinging around in a full circle, then allowing her to slide slowly down the length of his body to where he could gaze into the depths of her blue eyes before he sought out her lips. "I will always take care of you, my Maggie."

That night, sleep was impossible for Nicholas. His mind raced in endless swirls. It was hard to imagine being a married man, and even harder, being a father, but he would be a good one. Of that he had no doubt. Once they were married—the sooner, the better, for both of them—and he became eligible for a land grant, Maggie would most likely be allocated to him as a bond servant. At least that was usually the way it worked in New South Wales, and there was no reason to think it would be any different in Van Diemen's Land. Together they would cultivate a successful farm from the rich virgin earth and would have a wonderful life together with lots of children.

Chapter 23

Early the next morning, Nicholas wrote out his petition to Lieutenant-Governor Collins requesting permission to marry Margaret McKinnon, native of Ardnamurchan and convict sentenced to life. The papers were delivered the very same day.

That afternoon, Bowen still absent, David Long summoned Nicholas from his duty at the government garden. "There's trouble out back. Lieutenant Moore wants us up near the settlers' farms. There's a hoard of fully armed natives descending on us in a semicircle from the hills."

Nicholas abandoned the crowbar he had just driven deep into the unyielding soil and grabbed his jacket and musket from a nearby log. "How many are there? Did you see them?"

"At least three hundred, and Moore thinks they'll attack any minute."

They ran to the rear of the settlement, sweat already pouring from Nicholas' brow from digging. A short distance from Clarke's hut, they found Lieutenant Moore with a group of about ten corps men, all confused, uncertain of what to do next. Someone said the aborigines were hunting, driving a flock of kangaroos down the valley toward the stream, but the kangaroos were nowhere in sight by the time Nicholas and Long arrived.

Although armed with clubs and other objects, the natives passed Clarke's hut, leaving it undisturbed as they continued slowly across the valley toward the other huts. They made no move to attack, but their numbers were such that Moore feared for the safety of everyone. He was also acutely aware the situation provided an opportunity for him to show Bowen exactly what he was made of. His grip tightened around the gun lest the men notice his trembles. He must take command. Entrusted with the security of the settlement, he was not about to let himself or the corps down. Had these savages observed Bowen's departure and counted on finding the newcomers in a state of disarray, or was their arrival quite by chance? Whatever the case, he had his duty, a duty he would perform to the best of his ability.

"Load your muskets," he stated, in a voice betraying anxiety. "But don't fire until I give the order."

Scantily clad in animal skins, the aborigines passively watched the soldiers prepare for warfare, making no move as gunpowder was poured down the barrels of their weapons, then tamped down in readiness for the round bullet. Nicholas expecting them to seek cover or retreat, but then he realised they had no understanding of firearms.

Not even when the soldiers positioned themselves in two lines with the front row on its knees did they flinch or show any sign of fear. Then he noticed something; if these spear-carrying warriors had come to make war they would have left their families behind.

"Lieutenant," Nicholas called, from his kneeling position. "There are women and children out there."

"I can see that, Private," was Moore's flat reply as he moved to the right of the troop watching for the first sign of attack. If they made one threatening gesture, he would certainly give the order to open fire, meanwhile he prayed they would veer off or retreat up the hillside.

"We can't just shoot them, sir." Nicholas persisted, his musket trained on the closest warrior. "Aren't they just hunting kangaroos?"

"Better they die than any of us, so you will follow orders, Private Thomas, if I give the command to fire," the lieutenant retorted. "Disobedience won't be tolerated."

"Yes, sir," he replied, but Nicholas didn't like the idea of cutting down women and children. It was all too reminiscent of Rogers' tales, but if it came down to a them-or-us situation, he supposed he would have no qualms in pulling the trigger.

The screams of a panic-stricken Charlotte Burton who burst into view from behind her hut and dashed toward them brought Nicholas back to the present. With a babe in arms and another in tow, she shrieked at the aborigines to go away as another smaller group appeared behind her. Nicholas knew then he was capable of pulling the trigger.

At that instant Leo Turner and Moore's servant, John Cox, emerged from the trees with several small kangaroos slung across their backs. The sight of the dead animals enraged the aborigines and several of them ran up and formed a circle around the two hunters, trying to snatch away their catch. When the men protested, Turner most vigorously, the aborigines closed in, prompting terrified screeches from the trapped men.

"Fire over their heads," shouted Lieutenant Moore.

The thunderous volley did little to disperse the aborigines, who appeared only momentarily stunned before again closing in on the two men. Somehow Cox managed to scramble free on all fours and pelted toward the soldiers.

Unable to see exactly what was happening to Turner, Lieutenant Moore stepped forward. "You first five men come with me." Passing the fleeing Cox, the six scarlet-coated men ran up the slope to the foray, whereupon the aborigines released the apparently unharmed Turner, but steadfastly refused to relinquish the confiscated bounty, and the more the soldiers coaxed, the more obstinate the warriors became. Not wanting to lose face, Lieutenant Moore was about to use force when more yelling erupted from Burton's farm, where a smaller group had Walter Burton on the ground, imprisoning him similarly to Turner. As none of Turner's blood had been shed, Moore concluded they merely wanted to teach Turner a lesson rather than inflict any real harm, for had they intended otherwise, there was ample time for the savages to have murdered the man before Moore and his men reached them. But an uneasy Lieutenant Moore immediately dispatched David Long and Nicholas to Burton's assistance with instructions not to fire unless absolutely necessary.

It only took a matter of seconds for the pair to traverse the downward slope to Burton's farm, where he had managed to wrestle a club from one of his attackers. He swung it to fend them off and prevent his own small catch from being stolen. In defence, one of the warriors raised his club, and Nicholas heard Long's musket explode beside him before the aborigine dropped to the ground.

On hearing the shot, surgeon Jacob Mountgarrett, who'd been left back near Bowen's quarters to prepare one of the carronades in the event of a full-scale attack, fired the large-calibre gun at the marauders. Nicholas and Long nose-dove the instant they heard it, the flying pieces of metal sailing by, but the aborigines failed to react and many were struck by raining shrapnel. Petrified and dazed, they gathered their wounded and fled to the hills, many staggering, barely able to walk, but it was the pitiful wailing which most distressed Nicholas. He watched one poor man, moaning and mortally wounded in the chest, leave a trail of blood right up to the trees as he hung from the back of his rescuer. When they'd vanished, only the mournful wail of a small child, forgotten in their haste, remained.

After determining none of the settlers were injured beyond a few bruises, Jacob Mountgarrett, accompanied by a handful of soldiers and convicts, followed a trail into the valley beyond the settlement where five other bodies were found. Later, Mountgarrett dissected one of them for the entertainment of the officers and subsequently packed two boxes of bones to be sent off to Sydney for the benefit of his medical colleagues.

"What in God's name is Bowen doing?" roared Lieutenant Governor David Collins. "The man is never around when he's needed. Where is he this time?"

"Up the Huon somewhere after marooning eight men on an island," said the assistant. "Apparently they were found guilty of plotting to rob the store."

"Exploration is not this man's priority, discipline is," Collins thundered, as though his assistant were responsible. "He must have taken leave of his senses to strand men on some Godforsaken island while he goes gallivanting off on a whim.

And look what happens in his absence: a near massacre. It's inexcusable."

"I agree, sir," replied his always-calm assistant, appreciative of the lieutenant governor's utter exasperation.

Collins leaned back into the chair and for several moments sat staring, unseeing, at the papers on his desk. He then looked up and stated, "That child must be returned to its people forthwith and, as from today, I am placing the Risdon settlement under my direct command. See that the governor of Risdon Creek is informed of this immediately upon his return . . . whenever that may be."

Chapter 24

Some three weeks later, Bowen returned from the Huon River. When he approached his quarters, he was greeted by a gloomy-faced Lieutenant Moore hovering outside his equally sombre office. Following a brief exchange, a grey-faced Bowen led Moore inside whereupon he stepped toward his desk, hands clasped at his back. "When did you receive notice?" Bowen asked, with his back to Moore. He had not expected the news so soon, and certainly not while he was away. He turned and searched Moore's features for any sign of satisfaction, and finding only disappointment, he concluded Collins was perhaps considered underhanded in issuing such an order in his absence.

"It came early May, sir," Moore continued, "not long after an incident with the natives. That's what sparked it off, I understand . . . that, and your marooning the conspirators without first consulting the lieutenant governor then proceeding to an unauthorised exploratory expedition."

Bowen held up his palm. "Enough. Just tell me what happened with the blacks."

After Moore's briefing, Bowen demanded the two men involved in the shooting be sent in. "That won't be necessary, sir," Moore said, guessing the lieutenant governor's intention. "I've already written a report for Collins."

Bowen's face flushed. "You what?"

"He requested it, sir. I had no option."

Bowen withered into his chair. Not only had he been stripped of his command, but he and his entire settlement were banished from Van Diemen's Land as well. What would his family think? And his friends? Humiliated, he wished he was a million miles away. How could he ever hold his head high and look people in the eye again? But Collins had every right to be angry. The last thing the settlement needed was trouble with the natives. It went without saying, and he had to acknowledge this. Yet surely there was a way to salvage this execrable situation. How could he give up? He had worked too hard, endured too much, to let his efforts and his career simply slip away. There had to be something, some countermeasure by which he could reverse the situation. It would come to him eventually. These things always did. But for now, it was imperative he submit his own report.

Nicholas Thomas and David Long were swiftly brought to Bowen's quarters, along with the settler, Edward White, the first man to see the blacks approaching. Bowen's neck veins pulsated as they entered, and Nicholas thought the lieutenant governor was near collapse, but he rapidly regained his composure, making it clear that as far as he was concerned, the conflict with the blacks should have been avoided at all cost. "Our numbers are too few to survive a full-scale war that could result from this sort of thing, regardless of their primitive weapons," he said.

"The band was fully armed and entered the settlement uninvited," insisted Lieutenant Moore. "So I assumed they meant harm and gave the order to load the carronades and take arms, but I made it clear the men were to hold fire until I gave an order otherwise. It wasn't until the blacks attacked Burton that shots were fired."

Moore's version failed to sit well with Bowen. Until this incident, the natives had taken pains to avoid contact with the newcomers, so it could be assumed they were not predisposed to warfare. What, then, prompted the change?

Bowen turned to White, "Tell me in your own words what you saw."

"They were spread out, and I didn't see any spears, but they had clubs, and they appeared to be driving kangaroos down the valley toward the river, my guess was so the animals would be trapped there," White said. "When they saw me, they paused and stared awhile—a bit astonished at seeing me, I think—then they continued on. To me, they never seemed threatening, but I hightailed it down the creek to tell the soldiers, just to be on the safe side, sir, you know?"

"Then what happened?"

"I went back to work, hoeing new ground up near Clarkey's hut," White said. "By then the band had reached the hut," he continued, "and I was pretty much working in the middle of them as they moved on down toward the river."

"So you weren't afraid of them when they were all around you?"

"No, sir. Except for a few curious stares they ignored me. They never attempted to cross the creek or go near Burton's hut, and I didn't see them go into the camp itself either. From their manner, I'm pretty certain they would not have attacked the soldiers. They were more focused on hunting the kangaroos than on us, sir."

"So what sparked off the fight?"

There was a long pause during which David Long shifted his weight from one foot to the other. "It was hard to tell," he finally replied. "There was a lot happening; everyone was confused."

"It was Turner and Cox returning from a hunt, sir," Nicholas interjected. "The band didn't seem to like our hunters returning with a kill of a few small 'roos and got real angry, trying to take them. When the hunters resisted, a scuffle broke out, and a few soldiers, including the two of us, ran up to deal with it. About the same time, a confrontation involving Mrs. Burton occurred near her hut, and we got sent over there. Mr. Burton was about to be clubbed to death when a single shot dropped his would-be assailant. The next thing we knew, the carronade from down the hill had been fired and natives were running everywhere."

"Who fired the shot?" Bowen demanded.

"It was impossible to tell, sir," Nicholas said, aware Long was again shifting his weight back and forth beside him. "No one knows for sure."

Bowen's look of disbelief shot from one to the other. "Then what does everyone think? It must have been a topic of discussion." While Nicholas was wishing the incessant shuffling beside him would stop, Bowen bellowed, "For God's sake man, stand still and answer my question. Surely you have an opinion?"

"I couldn't point the finger at anyone," Long replied, fearful of Bowen's wrath.

"And what about you, Private Thomas, who do you think fired the shot?"

Nicholas cringed again at the thought of betraying his colleague and loathed the expectation he would deceive the governor. Instead he shot a pleading look in Moore's direction and shrugged his shoulders.

"Perhaps it's best not to speculate, sir," Moore interjected. "It's unfair to the men."

"Unfair, Lieutenant Moore?" said Bowen, barely concealing a sneer. "I would suggest that several events of late could qualify as *unfair*."

Moore gave a slight nod, but said nothing. Nicholas and Long likewise remained silent, the latter intently studying the newly formed hole in the toe of his dusty, scoured boot. Bowen released a long, low sigh, realising his pursuit of the matter, as usual, would be futile.

"Then in the interest of fairness and rectitude," he finally said, "we will take this up again in the morning after everyone has had sufficient time to reconsider their positions." He then looked directly at Nicholas. "You have disappointed me today, Private Thomas. I suggest you heed my last statement and review your recollection of the event."

But the next day Nicholas held to his story and later stood before Bowen for an entirely different reason.

Days before, when the news of Bowen's loss of command, along with the notification that his entire party was to return to Sydney Town became known, Nicholas had sought permission to join the ranks of Collins' party. Now he learned that this and his additional request for permission to marry in Van Diemen's Land had been denied, and he was to return to New South Wales with Bowen. "The reason," said a wry Bowen, staring down at the pile of papers that had accumulated in his absence, "is that Lieutenant Governor Collins considers it inappropriate for a soldier of the New South Wales Corps to remain in Hobart while ever there are marines present."

Nicholas tasted bile at the demolition of his world.

"Inappropriate?" he gasped, placing his hand on the desk to lean over and peer at the document before Bowen. "Wouldn't it be more inappropriate to leave a pregnant woman alone without a husband? What sort of an answer is that?"

"It's the only one sent, Private," Bowen said solemnly, his gaze shifting to the hand on his desk. "And may I remind you of to whom you are speaking?"

"Sorry, sir." Nicholas straightened to attention. "But it's not right. I can't leave her now. Her situation will be desperate, to say the least. Surely you can understand."

"After reading both your petitions, I am well aware of your predicament, Private Thomas, as is the lieutenant governor."

"Then you'll take up my cause, sir?" Nicholas said, grasping for any glint of hope. "Is there anything else I could do . . . resubmit the petition, perhaps? I just can't return to Sydney Town. What would become of her?"

"She'll go the way they all do, I expect. If you really cared for the woman, perhaps you should have thought about your situation before you bedded her," Bowen shrugged, his face betraying no emotion at the obvious parallel that could be drawn between himself and Martha Hayes. "There's nothing more to be done. You've had your answer. The decision is final."

"But—"

"That will be all, Private."

Nicholas was immobilised by disbelief. "But, sir—"

"I can do nothing."

The few moments before Nicholas was able to turn toward the door seemed an eternity, and as Bowen watched him cross the room, he scowled. How ironic that finally, when it was apparent to others that the corps and the marines were incompatible, lives and careers were left in tatters. Again he turned to the pile of documents on the desk, deciding in that instant that he would return to England and perhaps find a commission in India.

Chapter 25

The small boat slipped silently into the water with barely a ripple until Nicholas leapt aboard, sending a succession of waves to lap at the shore. He looked back up the hill scanning the sleeping settlement for any movement, fully aware that to any onlooker he would be easily seen under the full moon, but he knew once he was out on the water, the hovering river mist would quickly swallow him. He had spent many sleepless hours in reaching this decision, but it was a risk he was willing to take; he simply had to get to Maggie.

Once he was satisfied no one had stirred, Nicholas glided out midstream, taking care not to let the oars splash, and only when he was a good two hundred yards downstream and deep in the mist, did he to put his back into it, find a steady rhythm, and gain speed.

The night was cold, yet sweat soon dripped from his forehead as he powered downriver, without a thought for the consequence of desertion. His entire focus was on Maggie and how he had to be with her. Similarly, he did not consider any possibility that she may not want to run off with him.

He beached the boat a few hundred yards upstream of Hobart then stealthily made his way toward the settlement, cursing under his breath at each crunch or snap underfoot. Finally, from behind leafy camouflage, he surveyed the site, fully expecting to find only a few guards, definitely not the large number he discovered. There were two at Collins' quarters, two at the riverbank where the boats were moored, and several others stationed at various points nearer to where he crouched adjacent to the convict huts. Undoubtedly there were others out of view. Unlike Risdon they were everywhere, their occasional movement and intermittent mumbling indicating they were wide awake, leaving him no avenue of approach without detection.

Locating Maggie would have to wait until morning, so he retreated into the scrub to await the dawn and perhaps snatch a few hours' sleep. The grass was damp and uncomfortably cold in the thick undergrowth where he settled some fifty yards away, and he yearned for the blankets he'd stashed in the boat with the other provisions. It was going to be a long wait.

At some time, sleep must have found him for he awoke with a start as the settlement began to stir. Stiff and sore, he rubbed the circulation back into his hands and thighs then crept toward the activity. He placed a rock atop an old rotting tree stump as a signal to Maggie and settled back down to wait again. With the settlement's increasing hum of activity, he knew she would be out to tend the garden soon.

Maggie was easy to spot. Her long, dark hair was caught by the morning breeze and shone in the sun as she approached the garden, a shovel tucked under one arm while the other dragged a hoe. Eadie and the other women were equally laden, and it occurred to Nicholas that Maggie shouldn't be carrying so much, not in her condition, let alone toiling in the garden, but all that was about to end.

She noticed the sign almost immediately and slipped away within minutes, entering the bush at the rear of the camp, in the direction of the latrines, before circling back toward their usual meeting place. Nicholas intercepted her halfway and motioned her into silence. Moments later, they were hand in hand, running deep into the bush.

"I was so afraid you wouldn't come," she gasped. "Everyone's talking about Collins' plan to disband Risdon. Is it really true?"

"Yes," he said, now that they were far enough away to stop. "Everyone is to set sail for Sydney Town in early August—Bowen, his surgeon, the storekeeper, and all the corps. Of the entire camp, only thirteen convicts will be staying on at Hobart." Her face paled, and he took her in his arms. "But I'm not going to leave you. I have a plan, and I want us to leave here right now and go north. My old friend Buck told me about some sealing and whaling posts on the north coast. If we can reach one of them, it shouldn't be hard to get a working passage on one of the ships. Perhaps we can go to America or even back to Britain."

She pulled away, her bottom lip filling out. "How far is it to the north coast? I've about five months before my time, you know."

"It's less than two hundred miles. If we skirt the high country, it will be longer, but far easier going. I think we can do it in six, maybe eight, weeks. There are women at the camps, and they're sure to be skilled in childbirth, so there's nothing to fear. Besides, I'll never let you come to harm. You know that."

Maggie studied the familiar, well-formed features, his searching eyes suddenly etched with the fear that she might prefer to stay, as her mind raced toward weighing up the pros and cons. Certainly she had no inclination to giving birth in the middle of nowhere, but the notion of being without him was equally terrifying. "Well," she said eventually, "there's nothing for me here without you, so I'm game if you are. Let's make it a grand adventure to tell our grandchildren."

They both laughed. "That's what I love about you," Nicholas said, his voice a low rumble as he pulled her close. "You're always up for something new."

She responded to his kiss only momentarily before breaking free. "We'd best not waste time," she teasingly smirked. "Give me a few minutes to run back and get a few layers of clothing on, and anything else I can grab." After a quick squeeze of his hand, she was gone.

Within the hour, the two of them were well clear of the Hobart settlement. Along the way, they had retrieved the stash of supplies from the boat and now travelled inland to avoid any possibility of being spotted by someone from Risdon. As the sun climbed and warmed their skin, they walked hand in hand while the going was easy, but the undergrowth soon thickened and Nicholas had to push his way through, creating openings through which Maggie could follow as she fought with the skirts that caught on practically everything.

When they were well clear of both settlements and back on the banks of the Derwent, they took time to rest under a tall gum tree amid the hum of midday insects. The jutting point on the bank provided a panorama up and down the peaceful river, and Nicholas explained his plan to continue along its edge until they found shallows allowing them to cross, then they would head northward as best as the terrain would allow. He was not about to take Maggie into the high country. For one, the climbing would be exhausting, and two, the weather would cool with altitude, and they were unprepared for snow conditions. The possibility of becoming lost in the mountains was another deterrent.

The night was spent huddled together under blankets in a makeshift lean-to because Nicholas would not risk having a fire. Undoubtedly their absence had not gone unnoticed, and with the likelihood of a search party in pursuit, a fire glow would be seen for miles. They both welcomed the heat generated by the close proximity of their weary bodies which kept them cosy and allowed sleep to descend. Even the cries of night animals and their scuttling just outside the shelter failed to stir them.

Chapter 26

For five more days they hurried north, planning to slow the pace as soon as Nicholas was confident they had eluded any search party sent by Collins. From a distance, they hardly looked human, with various bundles of supplies strapped to their bodies. Nicholas had eventually caved in to Maggie's incessant pleading and agreed she could carry a portion of the clothing wrapped in a blanket that she secured over one shoulder in traditional Highlander fashion. Their provisions were meagre, but well thought out: a small quantity of salted beef, bread, a few utensils for cooking, and a large hunting knife which hung from Nicholas' belt. Even a tin containing tea leaves was tucked safely away in a pocket along with a flint for when it was safe to light a fire. Water was plentiful, with numerous clear streams to be crossed, and each time, they drank their fill. With his newly acquired hunting skills Nicholas knew that when the dried food ran out, he could provide fresh meat with the rifle and several shots he carried. They would not starve, of that he was sure.

Selecting the night's campsite, Nicholas dumped his load on the ground. Usually he chose a small clearing sheltered from the wind, and tonight was no different, except they were closer to the mountains and the site chosen had rocky outcrops on three sides. "Tonight we'll have a fire," he said. "We're far enough away not to be seen, even if they have followed us for a while."

"I was hoping you'd say that." For days Maggie had longed for the warmth of a campfire to ease her aching limbs, but determined not to complain, she prayed her body would soon become accustomed to the trek. Being from the Highlands where walking long distances was customary, she was normally strong, and it was frustrating to find herself so unfit. She put it down to being cooped up for months on end, first in prison and then on the ship. The fact that she was close to five-months pregnant did not feature in her reasoning. "How can you be sure we're always travelling north?" she asked, helping him gather scrub for the night's lean-to.

Until then it never occurred to him that she might doubt his judgement, although he sometimes questioned his own ability at times, not that he would ever admit it. Still, he was yet to be put to the test, but always he had reasoned that by keeping to the right of the mountains, they would eventually pass them and arrive at the northern seaboard, or Bass Strait as it was now called.

"If the sun always rises on our right side and sets on our left side, then we are facing north, and that's the general direction we've been heading," Nicholas replied. "Sometimes we turn slightly east or northeast, but that's so we skirt the high ground."

She shot him a wide-eyed glance as he draped an arm across her shoulders. "Generally we're going north all the time, so stop worrying. We should reach the north coast in a few more weeks," he said, praying he was correct. "Soon we'll have passed these mountains and the going should be easier, but it's also safe to slow down now, enough to catch our breaths, anyway."

"Praise the Lord," she laughed, rubbing her weary calves.

Nicholas studied her. Had he been pushing her too hard? The last thing he wanted was to cause her discomfort or harm her health in any way, but it was imperative they get as far from the Derwent as possible in the shortest amount of time to avoid capture. If they were caught, Maggie would undoubtedly be flogged, and he would more than likely face the firing squad for desertion. There was no choice but to push out hard at the start. Without complaining she had kept up all week, giving no indication how much her body ached until now. He had to admire her for that.

Nicholas crouched beside her. "Let me do it," he said, taking her legs across his lap and gently kneading the sore, tired muscles while she stretched out against the leafy ground-covering. For the first time, he became aware of the gentle swelling of her stomach and the reality of the child nestling within. At all cost, he would protect her and their unborn child. "The fire can wait a little longer," he said softly. "Let's get you comfortable first."

Later that night, he sat quietly watching Maggie, her features highlighted by the golden glow of the flames, and he felt a rush of warmth. She was everything to him now. He remembered the first time he saw her, lugging garden stakes about, and how his life had changed from that moment. She was the most beautiful and graceful creature he had ever known, yet it was her vitality, her love for life, and eternal optimism that captured his heart. Even the most oppressive situations never got the better of her for long, because it was a new life she was after, a better life, and together they would find it. Maggie gave purpose to his life and a newfound confidence. Not once had he doubted abandoning his army life, because with her anything seemed possible. He reached over, took her hand, and smiled into the familiar, Pacific-blue eyes. She responded with a squeeze, and if ever there had been a doubt, he knew now the decision to flee had been right.

Without warning and with great stealth, for neither of them heard a sound, the figure of a man was illuminated by the firelight. He was short, barefoot, clad only in animal skins, and his hair was covered in an ochre-coloured substance and braided into ringlets. In his right hand was a spear.

Maggie gasped as Nicholas lunged for his rifle, and as his eyes adjusted to peering past the fire into the orange gloom it cast, he made out several other similarly clad men in the background. Outnumbered, he froze, but not before training his barrel on the first man who stood his ground and surveyed the little camp, taking in every detail. Maggie scrambled to her feet beside Nicholas when, just as unexpectedly as they appeared, the men disappeared silently into the blackness.

Maggie clutched Nicholas' arm, her heart racing. "What do they want?" she cried. "Do you think they're going to kill us?"

"No, I don't think so," he said, still peering out into the night. "They had the chance if that's what was on their mind. My guess is they either saw or smelled our fire and came to investigate; they're just curious."

"Will they be still out there watching us?" Her eyes scanned the shadowy scrub beyond the campfire like those of a cornered cat.

"They'll have their own camp off somewhere. I'm sure they've seen all they needed to see here, otherwise they would have stayed longer, maybe even taken our food. I don't think they mean any trouble." Nicholas nevertheless placed more wood on the fire and stoked it so the surrounding area was well lit, ensuring there was a good supply for the remainder of the night. "I'd say they were probably watching us for a long time before deciding to show themselves."

A shiver spread through Maggie, and Nicholas found he had to extricate his arm from her frozen clutch before escorting her to the shelter erected earlier inside the tall, u-shaped rock formation. Despite his belief the aborigines were simply curious, there remained a small sliver of doubt, so he lay with one eye open, Maggie tightly in his arms and the rifle within easy reach. Should the aborigines decide to attack, he knew the two of them would never stand a chance.

"What was that stuff on their hair?" she murmured, at last sounding sleepy.

"Some sort of red paint," he replied. "Probably for decoration." Native Africans and Americans, so he had been told, painted their faces and bodies in various manners, usually to enhance their looks, but sometimes to scare the enemy. Obviously the red-ochre paint had made its impact on Maggie.

Chapter 27

At dawn the next day there was no sign of their visitors, so after swiftly gathering their belongings, they were on their way, both with an unnerving feeling of being watched. When Nicholas noticed Maggie's apprehensive surveillance of their surroundings, he said, "I'm sure the aborigines would never have attacked us at Risdon had we not fired first. Even when we aimed at them, it was obvious they didn't know what a gun was—you saw that last night—they were only interested in the kangaroos and catching food." He refrained from mentioning that they had tried to forcibly take the hunting party's kangaroo. "If we leave them alone, I'm sure they'll do likewise. We may never even see them again."

Nicholas was not so sure about this last statement, but wanted to give Maggie encouragement. Judging by her blanched face, she needed it.

It was not the last they saw of them. Although dark shadows were not often seen, and usually it was a mere fleeting glimpse through the trees that could have been the couple's imagination, they sensed the band's proximity, eventually drawing the conclusion that they had no desire to be seen. Certainly they posed no obvious threat and, as the days passed, both Nicholas and Maggie became accustomed to their ever-present aura.

It was three weeks after their departure from the Derwent, and Nicholas commented that John Bowen would have left for Sydney Town by now. "They were due to leave on ninth August, and it must be getting close to September by now," he said. As they walked along, he found himself considering how history might remember the first colonisation of Van Diemen's Land. If Collins had any say, it possibly won't be remembered at all, he thought, surprised at his own regret.

"That means the nights will be getting warmer," Maggie replied, her thoughts consumed by the miserable weather, nothing short of Highland temperatures, which they had encountered. But at least it was something she was used to, something she knew how to cope with, if grudgingly. All in all, things were not too bad, with Nicholas making sure they always had a fire, even carrying kindling wrapped in cloth under his coat to keep it dry in damp weather, her comfort never far from his thoughts. He made sure to catch something, however small, for dinner each day, although she suspected he loathed the killing their appetites demanded. Not once had she gone to sleep hungry.

Maggie was absorbed in her thoughts of what a good man Nicholas was when they were interrupted by the sight of a grazing kangaroo that had not yet heard their approach. With one swift and silent manoeuvre, he swung the rifle from his shoulder and aimed. No longer was there any hesitation in pulling the trigger. A thunderous crack filled the air, birds flew skyward, and the animal dropped.

"It'll be a heavy load, but it will keep us going for more than a week," Nicholas beamed, squatting as he paired off the last of the creature's hide, but Maggie's joy was silenced at the sight of several aborigines emerging from the trees behind him. One look at her face and he sprang to his feet, muscles taut and ready to face whatever would-be foe presented. Eight warriors swiftly surrounded them, the one wearing more necklaces than the others gestured toward the carcass and spoke words neither Nicholas nor Maggie understood.

"What do they want?" Maggie whispered, pressing against Nicholas' side.

"Our dinner, most likely."

Again, the leader pointed at the slain kangaroo, his voice louder than before, while another man moved to the side where Nicholas had left the gun on the ground and nudged the still warm barrel with a hesitant toe, which he withdrew with a mixture of fear and wonder. Clearly, these people had never seen metal before, and Nicholas surmised they had seen him shoot, but had no understanding of how the animal died. The man said something to the others who responded with a chorus of muttering, and one by one they moved closer to the weapon, peering at it suspiciously, but when Nicholas moved to retrieve it, a spear blocked his path.

Boldly, the leader grabbed the rifle from the ground, eyeing the barrel from each end and jiggled the trigger several times before deciding it was of little use and flung it under a nearby bush. He then turned back to the carcass. Without hesitation, Nicholas carved off a large section of the animal's huge thigh and indicated the band take the remainder. His action was greeted by another wave of muttering and a smile revealing a row of perfect white teeth from the leader, who nodded his understanding.

Immediately two men bound the animal's legs together, strung it onto a long tree branch, hauled it up between their shoulders and strode into the trees. Only as his gaze followed them did Nicholas become aware of several women and children, their hair cut close to their heads, standing well back and almost out of sight. Like the men, they were clad in animal skins, but without the red ochre hair adornment of their warriors, they were in stark contrast. Perhaps the clay was for protection he considered, given it gave the appearance of a helmet.

One women, with an infant partially concealed in the skins draped across her body, dashed forward and grabbed the newly peeled kangaroo pelt from the dirt, then hesitated, her attention on Maggie. Harsh sounds from one of the men sent her running back to the trees, but not before she cried out something, pointing at Maggie's belly. They all looked back, muttering again between themselves, and Nicholas felt a stab of fear at what kind of pagan ritual might prompt interest in a pregnant woman. The nearest man laid a hand on her stomach and uttered a confirmation to the others while Maggie, wide-eyed, looked questioningly at Nicholas. The man, whose eyes were darker than any man's she had ever seen, then abruptly turned and retreated back to the bush.

Alone again, they stood in silence, neither making a move until Nicholas decided to retrieve his rifle. It was Maggie who finally broke the silence. "Well, Nick," she said, "so much for your heavy load."

Chuckling, he returned to her side and took her in his arms. "Yours didn't go unnoticed either," he chided, denying the cold fist of fear twisting his stomach at the warrior's probing.

"Well, at least we still have something to eat," she shrugged,

"It's just as well I hadn't reloaded. That fellow would've blown his head off." Nicholas was still laughing as he regathered their provisions.

"I doubt we'd be here to joke about it if he had," she said, with sudden seriousness.

"Well, at least we know they don't mean us any harm, just don't appreciate anyone taking food they consider theirs."

Chapter 28

Weeks turned to months before Nicholas and Maggie saw the snow-covered mountains to the west—their constant companions—give way to hills, then undulating plains, and they were able to turn northwest toward the coastal sealing stations. They negotiated all types of terrain from steep slopes and rocky outcrops to low grassland and swampy marshes, and the going had been tough, but they were past the worst of it and both rejoiced when they finally encountered a river flowing north. Following it to the coast would be easy—at least that was what they thought—but the river meandered in one direction then another through country so rugged they soon had second thoughts. With sheer cliffs on both sides the scenery was spectacular. Surrounded by ferny cascades where the ground underfoot was damp and spongy, or deafened by tumbling waterfalls that misted the air and all but obscured the tree covered bank opposite, they laboured on, astonished by the breathtaking scenery at every turn. The ravine stood in stark contrast to the land recently traversed. Under other circumstances, they may have stopped for a day or two to take it all in, but sheer determination drove them on, both feeling an urgency to push forward. Only when they found themselves at the bottom of a seemingly endless chasm did Nicholas concede it was useless to continue.

Maggie, now too heavy with child to traverse back up the demanding chasm again if they were forced to retrace their steps, needed a safe place to stop and rest. After finding a small cave-like shelter beneath a rocky outcrop near the base of one of the falls, Nicholas left her while he went in search of a safe way through the cliffs. Two days later he returned, a small wallaby swinging from his belt. He'd found a way out, but it was too late to start, so they spent the evening on a long, flat rock by the deep pool created eons ago by torrents of water gushing from the rocky ledge above while fresh meat roasted over their nearby fire.

The evening was warm, probably mid-November by Nicholas' calculation, and everything seemed perfect—everything, except for the fact that their trek had taken them far longer than anticipated. He had thought by now they would be at the coast with Maggie in the care of some sealer's wife skilled in childbirth. A pang of guilt edged with fear squeezed his gut. Her time was only a matter of weeks away. It was imperative they reach the north coast soon.

"I missed you these last two days," she said, breaking the silence. "Waiting here gave me a chance to rest, but it was lonely without you."

"But you didn't doubt I'd be back, did you?" he said, thinking she must have been afraid. It was a thought that sometimes lingered in the back of his mind, but he'd never really focused on it because his prime concern was always that they had shelter, enough food, and sufficient wood to keep the fire burning. Still, he never wanted her to be afraid of anything.

"Of course. I never doubted that. I was just lonesome." She lay on her side, her head against his thigh, gazing across the water. "You do grow on a person after a while, you know."

When he laughed, Maggie twisted around to meet his eyes. Her look was that of a caress, prompting a familiar surge of warmth through his body, and he knew then she'd had no fear. She trusted him completely; he could see it in her eyes. Still, he wondered if he would prove worthy of that trust and prayed that he would be. Studying her features, serene in the fire-glow, he leaned closer and whispered, "You're the most precious thing in the world, my Maggie." His lips brushed hers as his hand cupped her cheek. "You mean everything. You'll always be safe with me." Yet somewhere inside, he knew his words were more for his own benefit than hers.

He saw in her a strong, determined Highland woman, who knew exactly what she wanted and was prepared to fight for it. Only her condition prevented her long, muscular legs and supple, healthy body from carrying her toward their goal. Not one of the women he'd known in Kent would have put up with what Maggie McKinnon had silently endured these past months, and even now, despite being eight months pregnant, she remained as mentally strong and determined as ever, perhaps even more so. He stroked her long, thick, dark hair, knowing he was very blessed.

Within a week of leaving the torturous river terrain, Nicholas and Maggie were again heading northwest through gently sloping hills when, much to their amazement, they were confronted with what appeared to be a road. To be precise, it was more like a wide track, the vegetation burnt to keep it open. They had encountered a similar, although narrower, trail of burned undergrowth several weeks ago, but at the time, Nicholas had assumed it was caused by lightning. This second example convinced him the trail was definitely manmade. It was too well marked out, running in an almost perfect east-west direction, to be the result of nature. Undoubtedly it was aborigines who had set it alight to keep the undergrowth at bay. It was probably used for seasonal migration, he surmised, and despite the track being a much easier route to travel, Nicholas could not risk further delays in getting to the coast by following it. Disappointed, he led Maggie to the far side where they resumed their northerly journey. Again they felt eyes watching their every move, but as usual saw no one.

With Maggie heavily pregnant, they paced themselves slowly, only walking half the miles they should have covered. From the way she repeatedly slowed to rub her lower back, Nicholas knew she was in pain. He stopped to set up camp for the night earlier and earlier, and soon they were only walking a few hours each day. At every hilltop, he would search the horizon for the coast, a glimpse of ocean.

There was never anything but trees.

Chapter 29

The contractions came at regular intervals and were now more frequent. When the pain first gripped Maggie, some twelve hours earlier, they immediately stopped so Nicholas could construct a shelter. This time it was not a lean-to he built amid the trees. It was a crude structure consisting of two sides and a roof fashioned from long sticks through which he wove shorter branches to form the walls around her. Then he collected water from a nearby stream and lit a fire. Back home, childbirth always required boiling water. Next he cut two lengths of twine in readiness to tie the cord when the baby was born then placed his knife in the boiling water so it would be clean when it came time to sever the cord. After this, he joined Maggie under the shelter and waited.

From time to time, Nicholas wiped the sweat from her forehead with a cool cloth rinsed in the stream while her grasp with each contraction all but crushed his hand. Never had Maggie imagined childbirth to be like this . . . so painful . . . and try as she might, her usual calm evaporated into frenzied sufferance. Each contraction caused an involuntary cry, over which she had no control, and as day turned to night, her agonising howls continued to pierce the silence.

Nicholas tried to steel himself against her cries, but it was no use, they were like a knife paring his heart open, and there was little he could do, save cradle her head in his lap and let her rent his hands when the pain gripped her body. As the hours wore on, he began to fear something was terribly wrong and, feeling utterly helpless, wished he had paid more attention to the birth of his father's farm animals. Having heard of breech births, where the baby came out backward, he knew nothing of how to remedy the situation if, in fact, their baby was in the breach position. Certainly there was no head to be seen. Or was it just still too high up? Nicholas had no idea.

"You're doing fine, darling," he whispered onto her moist forehead, stroking her sweat-laden hair. "It'll be over soon."

Maggie merely gasped, "Hope so", before her panting resumed. Surely the pain could not last much longer. No one would ever have children if this sort of suffering was normal. And it was not normal, of that she was convinced. Fear began to give way to panic, but she lacked the strength to express it. All she knew was she could not take much more. Clutching Nicholas' hands, she closed her eyes, all thought stifled by yet another contraction.

By morning little had changed. There was still no sign of the baby's head, and the contractions continued. Maggie was in a state of utter fatigue, barely able to swallow the water Nicholas offered between her panting and moaning. The once robust shrieks were now weary, pitiful moans. They both knew this disastrous situation could have calamitous results.

In desperation, Nicholas attempted to turn the baby by manipulating it from the outside, but as soon as he applied pressure to her swollen belly Maggie cried out in even greater agony. He didn't try again for fear of doing greater damage, especially as he was unsure of what he was doing in the first place, and he couldn't stand the thought of increasing her pain. They would just have to wait it out.

The hours wore on with little change. Maggie's strength ebbed before his eyes, and Nicholas came to the horrifying realisation she might die. She was slipping away, and he was powerless to do anything but hold her. So he cradled her in his arms and gently rocked her while stroking her pallid cheeks, offering what little comfort he could, as he stifled the sobbing within.

How long the dark figures had been there he had no idea, but suddenly Nicholas was aware of movement outside the shelter. They must have heard Maggie's cries and come to investigate. The men made no movement toward him, and he remained motionless, his arms firmly around Maggie, until someone finally pushed through from behind. A woman, wrinkled with age and wearing only a loose, kangaroo-skin cape, stooped low, and entered the shelter. Kneeling beside Maggie, she murmured words he could not understand while reaching up under Maggie's skirt. Fearful of her intentions, Nicholas' immediate reaction was to push the woman away, but Maggie stirred with the movement, and the woman's other bony brown hand stroked her forehead. The trace of a welcoming smile crossed Maggie's exhausted face, and Nicholas realised there was nothing to fear.

The woman put her ear to Maggie's exposed stomach and nodded, again saying words neither understood, while another woman, younger than the first, brought in a large sea shell containing a murky-looking fluid. This she gave to Maggie who unreservedly gulped the dark potion down. Next the two women began hovering over Maggie, removing her already loose skirt and probing. Nicholas was motioned to leave, and again he felt the grip of fear and refused to go. What if she needed him? While still cradling her head and shoulders in his lap, the two women began manoeuvring, one from the top and one from between Maggie's legs. When she cried out in pain, flailing her arms at them, they pushed her hands away and eventually the second woman, kneeling closest to Nicholas, placed Maggie's hands into his, and he understood he was to hold them, preventing further interference.

Maggie's protests became screams ignored by the women who continued their manipulation between contractions. After what seemed an eternity, they sat back, seemingly satisfied, and Nicholas surmised the baby was at last in the right position. At the same time Maggie's cries increased along with her pushing and finally, between her legs, appeared the baby's blood-streaked head. The older woman held up a hand indicating Maggie should stop pushing, but all her efforts for the past two days had been directed toward expelling this child; there was no way she could stop. As the baby's shoulder began to appear the woman hooked a finger under its arm and with the next push lifted the wailing, blood-covered baby free and placed it, cord still pulsating, on Maggie's chest.

"It's a boy," Nicholas said, as Maggie, too exhausted to reply, placed a protective hand across the infant's back and smiled weakly up at Nicholas, whose little finger was in the grasp of the child's tiny hand. "Finally, you have arrived, my son," he whispered.

Nicholas gazed lovingly at the child, the beautiful, perfect, healthy boy Maggie now held, thanks to the women who seemingly had nothing to gain by their actions. If he ever had questions as to their motives, they were swamped by his ecstasy as the cord was tied and cut by the older woman who then wiped the child clean and put him to Maggie's breast. Nicholas watched, fascinated, as the tiny mouth sought her nipple and began sucking, feeling a sense of pride and power. Here was his family and his future, the three of them. Nothing could ever stop their dreams coming true, not after the ordeal they'd both just survived.

"We'll name him Buck after my American friend, Buck Jones, the whaler," Nicholas said, stroking the child's flaxen wisps of hair. "He will be Buck William Thomas. William was my father's middle name. It's a good, strong name, and he will grow up to be just that: good and strong."

Maggie was not too sure about the name, preferring a traditional Scottish name like Donald or Angus. What sort of a name was Buck, anyway? But she was too tired to protest. Besides, she was happy just to have the child in her arms rather than her belly, and the joy in Nicholas' eyes was unmistakable. Nothing else mattered right now. All she wanted to do was sleep.

Nicholas took her hand in his, gently kissing her fingers, and as their eyes met she smiled, her face once again serene, before closing her eyes. Only then did he become aware of the growing pool of blood between Maggie's legs.

On his knees, Nicholas shuffled down her side as the younger woman scrambled to a position opposite him. Under the older woman's direction, she commenced massaging Maggie's stomach while the other applied gentle, continuous tension to the cord in an attempt to dislodge the placenta. All the while, blood seeped through her clothing onto the grass.

Nicholas was gripped by panic. "Can't you stop the blood?"

They had no understanding of his words, but it was apparent they understood his meaning.

"For God's sake, stop the bleeding," Nicholas cried again, glancing up at Maggie who stirred only slightly under the pressure of the woman's hands. He shuffled up to place her head on his lap again, being careful not to dislodge the still suckling child.

The women continued their attempts to remove the placenta by applying direct tension to the cord and massaging the stomach. Finally it came away. The older one inspected it thoroughly while the other continued massaging. If the womb could be stimulated to start contracting back to its normal size, the flow of blood would decrease. Once the examination of the placenta was complete, the older woman indicated part of it was missing, still inside Maggie, and this was causing the haemorrhage. The younger woman moved aside as the older took over the massaging.

It made no difference. Blood continued to spill onto the ground. Nicholas again took Maggie's hand as he stroked her damp hair. It was cool to the touch. With horror, he saw her other hand fall from the child at her breast, and seconds later, the boy was wailing pitifully. Gripped by panic, Nicholas shook her, "Maggie! Wake up. For God's sake, wake up!"

The child rolled to one side and was caught by the younger woman before he struck the ground. Maggie remained unresponsive, her eyelids slightly parted and eyes unseeing.

He didn't know how long he stayed there with her, cradling her lifeless, cold body in his arms. Nor did he know or care where his child was. None of that mattered now. He had loved this woman as few men love a woman. With her, life had been a constant joy, filled with promise. Losing her now was more than he could bear. The future would be bereft of the shared aspirations, trials, and joy their life together should have held and existing without her—for a mere existence is what that life would be—seemed intolerable. His heart felt wrenched from his chest, leaving a gaping, cavernous hole that nothing would ever fill again, and as the cool of the night air settled upon them, Nicholas felt a blackness envelope him as never before.

Chapter 30

When dawn broke Nicholas was still awake, still holding Maggie. The aborigines remained nearby, camped a little further back from the stream. They soon began to stir and move about, but made no move to leave, as though waiting for something. By midmorning Nicholas knew it was time to bury Maggie, but he couldn't bear to let her go, and when various band members pointed to the trees, he ignored them until a woman took him by the hand and tugged him to his feet. She led him into the bush for several hundred metres, the others following, and stopped at a hollowed-out tree. Nicholas was confused until recalling stories of the tribes' practice of laying their dead to rest in hollow tree stumps. He shook his head and turned away.

Recalling Maggie's love of water, Nicholas chose a high piece of ground overlooking the stream where, to the amazed utterances of the aborigines, he began to dig. The ground was hard, embedded with small rocks, and the sticks with which he was forced to improvise frequently broke, yet he kept at it, sometimes even using his bare hands. Maggie would have a proper grave if it was the last thing he did.

When at last the hole was deep enough, he took one long last look at her ashen, but still beautiful face and cut off a long lock of her hair, placed it in his breast pocket, then tenderly wrapped her in one of the blankets. As Nicholas gently laid his beloved Maggie to rest in the grave, the muttering among the aborigines told him they had never seen a person buried in this manner before.

The echoing tap of the first sprinkling of earth onto the blanket brought forth a wave of desolation, and Nicholas fell to his knees. In a frenzied effort to regain control, he pushed more earth toward the grave. Surely he had shed all the tears he was capable of overnight, yet his body shook uncontrollably and he found himself dry retching as the earth tumbled into the hole.

With the grave finally filled, he fashioned a cross from twisted branches and placed it ceremoniously upon the mound before kneeling and praying for the first time in many years. Tears streamed down his face as the aboriginal band remained in the background, silently watching the display of emotion.

It must have been well past midday when the young woman who assisted at the birth appeared beside the kneeling Nicholas, his son, snugly wrapped in kangaroo hide, in her arms. The child had Maggie's blue eyes and his own fair hair and was pale and fragile against the woman's skin. He should feel some emotion toward the boy, and he felt guilty that he could find none. Maggie had given her life for the boy, but his feelings were now spent, leaving nothing for the child.

The woman seemed to understand as she delved into his eyes and placed a comforting hand on his shoulder. The words she uttered were lost on him, but the pressure of her hand urged him to follow as the band turned toward the trees. For a long moment, he hesitated, staring down at the crude grave, then inexplicably he was drawn toward his son. It was as though the boy called to him . . . or was it Maggie urging him to follow? Either way, he knew what he must do. He took one last look at what was left of his love then trudged after the aborigines.

Her name was Skylamahana, and she'd been suckling Buck for the past week. She'd recently lost her own child and her husband in a battle with another tribe and was eager to care for the new little baby whose skin was so fine and pale. He wondered if it was Skylamahana who drew the band's attention to Maggie's pregnancy all those months ago. He recalled that woman having a small child with her.

Normally their band, the Pallitteeler, being part of the northern tribe, didn't venture so far south at that time of year, but this last winter they sought retribution for the destruction of their spirit tree by the Lummeraiggair band, and this took them further south than normal. It was during the ensuing battle that Skylamahana's husband was killed. Soon after, the cold took her baby, leaving her with a son of about five years and a daughter of about three.

Skylamahana was the daughter-in-law of Warcottewilda the midwife and had been training under the older woman's guidance since her marriage. It was expected she would take over the role of midwife when the older woman was no longer able. Skylamahana was a fit and able woman. Under her care, little Buck thrived, but not so Nicholas. He loved his son, yet could find little joy in living, Maggie's loss and his guilt leaving him drained of vitality and will. He lost weight, his eyes became sunken, and his skin sallow. In his darkest hours, he wished for death, yet somehow, miraculously, he kept going.

The band wandered about the country in search of food in, what seemed to Nicholas, an aimless pattern, and still there was no sign of the coast, although he understood they would be going there soon. For now, the band was intent on hunting in this particular location because it was the right season to do so. He gradually learned of their well-established patterns of seasonal migration and hunting. It would be a week or so before they would travel to the coast. Repeatedly, Nicholas considered taking Buck and setting off by himself, but the infant wouldn't survive without breast milk, so he resigned himself to remaining with the band until the child was weaned before leaving to search for a sealer's camp.

Chapter 31

Days turned to weeks, and Nicholas' guilt and grief became no easier to endure. Not a day went by without him agonising over his decision to bring Maggie into the wilderness with the promise that she would be safe, that he would always take care of her. He had let her down; it was that simple, and now she was gone. If it were not for the aborigines he too would have perished, for he had little will to live. Yet despite his misery, some unknown force compelled him to survive, and he remained with the Pallitteeler band, joining their annual migratory pattern. He saw no evidence of them having any knowledge of agriculture, their existence being totally based on hunting and gathering. In doing so, they made implements of stone, wood, and bone of very simple design. Metal was unknown to them, hence their continued fascination with Nicholas' knife and rifle, even though he had long since run out of ammunition.

They made their stone tools by flaking off small pieces of one stone by hitting it with a larger stone until a sharp edge was formed. These tools were never mounted on a handle, and when Nicholas demonstrated how to make axes and knives by wedging stone into wood and binding it firmly into place with leather thongs, there was much interest. But later, when the implements were put to the test during a hunt, the men became frustrated by their lack of dexterity and soon reverted to their old methods. Practice, it became apparent, was something the mature hunters were not willing to spend time on, but the younger women and children persisted and soon became quite deft with an axe.

Work was strictly divided between men and women. Hunting was the men's domain, while gathering and cooking was left to the women who were also responsible for carrying the children and most of the men's possessions when they were on the move, leaving the hunters burdened with only spears and perhaps a waddy. Pallitteeler cooking consisted solely of roasting over a fire. They had no pottery of any kind and were unable to boil water.

Fire was the band's most precious possession. Since they had no way of making it themselves, a burning stick was carried with them wherever they went and tended with the utmost care to ensure it remained alight. If they were unfortunate enough to lose the flame in wet weather, they had no choice but to either beg some from a friendly neighbouring band or wait for lightning to strike a fire. Because of his flint stone, Nicholas changed all this for the Pallitteeler. He could strike a flame in almost any kind of weather, so the burden of the fire carrier was greatly relieved and no longer was there anxiety and despair if the flame happened to die. It gave freedom such as they had never known and elevated Nicholas' status within the group.

Hunting spears were plain wooden lances, without barbs or stone points, fashioned usually from long, slender tea-tree stems that had been planed by a sharp-edged stone so they spun during flight. For such a simple implement, they were remarkably accurate and quite deadly at less than one hundred yards. Nicholas had witnessed many a kangaroo brought down at distances he was sure the hunter would miss, and he developed great respect for their skills. Their other weapon, the waddy, was a wooden club with one end bluntly pointed and the other roughened for a good hand-grip. It could be either thrown or used to strike a battering blow at close quarters.

Chisel-like sticks were the tools of choice used by the women to dig roots and, when at the seashore, collect abalone and raid the burrows of mutton-birds. These were also excellent for prising sheets of bark from trees for use in the construction of their shelters—another female responsibility—and cleaning animal hides in readiness for their fashioning into capes and other items of adornment. Many men wore fine animal sinews adorned with small ochre-coloured beads about their necks, while the women preferred strings of small shells or narrow strips of fur.

Nicholas found he enjoyed learning Pallitteeler custom and language, for they provided distraction from his painful thoughts and ever-present guilt. Soon he was able to communicate at a basic level in their language and they picked up several English words. Of particular interest were the words for which their own language had no equivalent, words like shirt, flint, gun, and knife.

The Pallitteeler was not a large band. It consisted of eight family groups of three, and sometimes four, generations led by Manekedru, the strongest hunter, rather than one of the older and wiser men. Age and wisdom were respected, but greater emphasis was placed on superior hunting and fighting prowess.

Nicholas learned that marriages were usually arranged

by the parents of a child reaching puberty with a member of another band or tribe. Usually the pair remained together for life, and because Skylamahana was suckling his son, the band expected him to assume the role of her husband. At first he was repulsed by the idea. There was no way he could be with another woman after his Maggie. His heart and soul still ached for her. He craved one more look at her beautiful, smiling face and to hear the sound of her laughter once more. He was haunted by dreams of running his fingers through her thick, dark hair and breathing in its sweet fragrance. He felt none of this for Skylamahana, only gratitude, but this was not what she and the band wanted or expected. Certainly the woman was kind and capable, but she could never replace Maggie; the mere thought plunged him to the depths of despair.

Instead he busied himself with adapting to Pallitteeler customs in other ways, even smearing his body with a mixture of grease and ochre to keep warm when his clothes became threadbare and began to disintegrate. This mixture, plus a fur cape draped across the shoulders and a fire, was all they used to keep warm. Such simple measures served them well, but Nicholas still felt the cold and retained a blanket, wearing it highland fashion as Maggie had shown. To this, he added a fur cape and tied skins around both feet for warmth and protection. The band considered shoes an odd custom. There had been much amusement at his efforts to repair his boots when they were falling apart, and later, when the boots were beyond salvaging and he proceeded to bind his feet, there was outright hilarity. Thousands of years of adapting to Van Diemen's Land's temperature and terrain gave them no need for such protection.

Although agreeable to smearing his body with grease, Nicholas drew the line at having a similar substance loaded onto his hair so it could be twisted into narrow, tubular ringlets that were left to hang like a mop, all but obscuring the eyes, as worn by the other men. Even though his hair was now well past his shoulders, he preferred to tie it back at the nape, English fashion, leaving his vision totally unobscured.

With practice, he became a good marksman with the spear, but when the band hunted he was never the one to make the kill. Always one of the other men, usually Manekedru, who was far more skilled with the weapon than Nicholas' new-found dexterity allowed, would step in. Nevertheless, he was a useful hunter, gaining respect for his stealth and patience during the hunt and his physical endurance during a chase. Possessing greater muscle mass than the wiry aborigines, he was, to their astonishment, often able to lift heavier weights with ease, but it was his ability to light fire that was most valued. And so it was that Nicholas became a welcome addition to the Pallitteeler, while he, unbeknownst to them, waited for the day he and his son would leave.

Chapter 32

Months rolled by with no sign of a sealing party, and Nicholas became impatient. The band visited the coast, hunted and returned inland. According to custom, they congregated at the mouth of a great river with other bands from the Northern tribe to gather eggs and hunt the variety of water birds that nested there each year.

At night, by the campfire, Nicholas absorbed every detail he could of numerous stories relayed about white sealers and their seasonal settlements to the west, recognizing such knowledge would one day prove useful.

But not all the tales were good, and for the first time, he found himself cringing at the colour of his skin. The bands were now forced to avoid many of their traditional hunting grounds during the sealing season because of the white man's propensity for aboriginal women. Most were not above stealing a girl for an evening's entertainment, and it was not unknown for some of the more attractive ones to be forced into a lifetime of slavery. He was appalled that his own kind could abuse these kind, gentle people.

From all accounts, the sealer settlements were small, with only an occasional hunter bringing his wife along to make their shack a little more homelike. Usually the men were dropped off somewhere along the coast with meagre equipment and provisions then picked up by the same vessel at the end of the season. It was a harsh and rugged life, but they took to the challenge, revelling in their hardy reputation.

Despite memories of Maggie, there were times when Nicholas, too, yearned for the touch of a woman, but after these stories he found himself fearful of the band's reaction. They had always been sympathetic to his loss, many having experienced something similar, but for them life went on. The quicker things returned to normal, the better for the entire group. Nicholas always resisted their urging, clinging to the past, refusing to be led astray, as he saw it. Yet now, when he found himself able to rationalise, and despite the band having made it clear that they considered it time he moved past his tragedy, he still feared being likened to the sealers. Would they now think he was capable of abusing their women? Self-conscious, he found himself withdrawing, but days passed with no one treating him differently or indicating he was any less valued.

After a time, his self-imposed alienation dissipated, and he returned to his usual activities with the band. As his confidence returned, so did his desire. Most of the women were already spoken for, leaving only a few very young women, children in Nicholas' eyes, and the widow, Skylamahana. He knew everyone would be pleased if he took up with her, but somehow it still didn't seem right.

There could be no denying he was fond of the pleasantly featured Skylamahana and, over months, had softened to the once-foreign high cheekbones, small, broad nose, and full lips concealing strong, white teeth. Even the way the women cropped their hair was beginning to have its appeal, but it was her soft, dark eyes, set so widely apart, that bespoke her true being. She was a goodhearted, compassionate person, who cared for his son admirably and indicated her desire to serve Nicholas in a more intimate way many a time, but he'd always turned her away. Undeterred, she'd persisted in regarding him as her husband, catering to his every need and doting on the child until at length Nicholas' physical needs were such that he could resist no more. Taking Skylamahana as his woman, he allowed himself to become lost in the welcoming soft, warm cradle of her embrace, and for a few moments as he soared to the heavens, he forgot his beloved Maggie.

There was already movement in the camp when they rose at dawn to be greeted by Warcottewilda's laughter followed by a dry comment about how it was high time they got around to consummating their relationship. Somewhat embarrassed, Nicholas busied himself with the morning chores while Skylamahana, far from disconcerted, simply smiled her acknowledgment, obviously pleased with the new arrangement; she again had a husband.

Her feelings for Nicholas grew quickly, and she demonstrated her affection in the many ways she waited on him and welcomed him into her arms every night. Likewise, he developed greater affection for her, but knew he could never love her as he had Maggie. Although he'd come to better understand Pallitteeler culture, there remained an invisible chasm between them. Even her name was a problem. Being too much of a mouthful, he tried to shortened it to the more familiar Hannah, which she failed to recognise as referring to herself, but she did respond to Skyla, mainly just to please him, so from then on that was what he called her.

Nicholas enjoyed running his hands over her soft, slick skin in the evenings when they sat around the fire, his hand repeatedly drawn to the intricate pattern of raised scars in the form of tiny, little dashes that ran across her back, shoulders and upper chest. All but a few adults displayed some kind of pattern on their bodies, never the children. The scars were etched in several rows forming a garland effect and were soft, yet firm to the touch, and he inquired on many occasions how they were made, only to be told he would see with his own eyes soon enough.

That winter the son of Papomenelya, a tall boy called Minnalargolga, reached puberty, and as was the custom, the young man was to receive his cicatrices, the body decorations that so fascinated Nicholas. They were made by cutting designs directly into the skin then rubbing a mixture of powdered charcoal, red ochre and grease into the open wounds. The result was permanent scarring in the form of raised weals. Minnalargolga, eager to attain the mark of adulthood, presented himself without any sign of fear. The entire band gathered ceremoniously as Noolengwanna, the skilled artist of countless rites, commenced slicing the boy's skin with a blade-sharp stone. Not once did Minnalargolga cry out or exhibit any hint of discomfort, for to do so would bring instant shame on himself and his family. Blood streamed from the wounds, but this failed to deter the boy or the artist. Noolengwanna deftly, but with great concentration, cut his pattern of repeated dashes and circles into the boy's chest then continued across his shoulders, upper arms and back before discarding the stone implement in favour of a shell containing a dark, greasy mixture that he proceeded to rub into the wounds. It was this last process that was crucial to the formation of weals. Miraculously, the boy still did not flinch.

This rite was not only reserved for boys passing into manhood. Women like Skyla proudly wore cicatrices of a different design, their patterns being representative of the band or tribe into which they were born. In the past, Nicholas had considered the rite a barbaric custom, yet now he watched the proceedings until they were complete. Then Minnalargolga, now a man, simply rose and, along with the rest of the band, went about their usual business. There was no other celebration of passage.

By far the most disturbing Pallitteeler custom in Nicholas' eyes was that of wearing the jawbone of a dead friend or loved one hanging from a thong or grass twining around their neck. Not everyone wore a jawbone, but several men did, including Manekedru who, being a friend of Skyla's late husband, displayed his jawbone in fond memory. Nicholas never learned what the dead man's name had been, because to utter it after death was taboo. When Linkaroomaga, a woman of countless years, died, the entire band gathered wood to form an enormous funeral pyre. Onto this was placed the body of the woman, her face to the east, her legs and arms bent up against her body and bound firmly into position. The pyre was then set alight and tendered by the solemnly watching band until only bones remained. Her son retrieved the jawbone, and her remaining bones were placed in a hollow tree, after which the family then rubbed themselves with ash from the fire to ward off evil spirits. Pallitteeler customs were often bizarre from an English perspective, and yet they were a gentle people whom Nicholas grew to respect and admire.

Food was the centre of their existence, and their focus was on the family unit, then their band, followed by the tribe. The Pallitteeler were part of the Northern tribe. Their days were spent migrating along well-defined routes within their territory in search of food. They endeavoured to maintain good relationships with the North-Western, the North Midlands and the Big River tribes, and the Pallitteeler had permission to enter their hunting territory in exchange for access to the ochre mines of the Northern tribe. When there was no warfare, they were generally happy in their harsh existence, despite its many taboos and fearful evil spirits.

Nicholas was surprised to learn they did not worship a particular god, but great effort was spent in avoiding devils. When someone died that particular site became taboo and would never be visited again. Perhaps this was why the band had been so alarmed when he buried Maggie near the stream—that, and him placing her under the ground, something they could never comprehend.

Likewise, he had misgivings about the superhuman beings the band associated with the stars, but he enjoyed the stories told by the elders, along with the tribal legends they passed on to the children through song and dance. Being the band's future, the young were always well treated and showered with affection. They had great freedom and were able to do almost as they pleased, but a stern hand was available when necessary. Mostly the children spent their time imitating their elders and acquiring skills to use later in life. There was little time set aside for play except in the evenings, but as all children will, they made a game of almost any task.

And soon there would be a new child to become a custodian of these teachings—the one now nestled deep within Skyla.

Chapter 33

In the spring of 1805, Skyla prepared to give birth to Nicholas' child. Custom decreed she be left behind with Warcottewilda when the time of birth drew near, allowing the band freedom to continue their hunt unhindered. The woman's husband, considered too valuable a hunter, never remained behind, leaving the mother, carrying her newborn babe, to catch up as best she could. Memories of Maggie caused Nicholas to refuse to go on without Skyla, and so the band left, muttering their disapproval.

The pains of labour, despite Skyla's gritted silence, brought back Maggie's agony all too clearly, but it was an easy birth, and the pains were quickly forgotten upon the arrival of a healthy, wailing boy, whom Nicholas named Lucas after his own father. The boy had his mother's dark, doe-like eyes and deep-caramel skin. Had Nicholas known the birth was to be uncomplicated, perhaps he would not have created such a fuss at the thought of leaving her behind. Skyla astonished him, taking everything in her stride, even the rush to be again on the move. To her, it was the natural way of things and always would be, so within the hour, the trio was mobile again.

In time, the band arrived at the coast and again congregated with the other bands of the Northern tribe at the river mouth to gather fresh eggs. It was a season of bounty with swans and ducks in plentiful numbers and their eggs easily procured. Even the warmer weather made getting seafood a pleasant pastime, and the children enjoyed splashing about in the shallows while the women looked for shellfish.

Young Buck was well able to sit up by himself and was fast becoming an active crawler, causing Skyla to be ever watchful when he ventured near the water. The lively handful thrived under her doting care at the expense of her other two children, Manseleema and Iakondratta, who, although they performed their duties as older brother and sister of this remarkable blond, blue-eyed little boy, were sometimes resentful. With the sudden death of their father and the formation of a new family unit upon the arrival of Nicholas and Buck, Skyla knew their adjustment would be difficult and many times sought to give them extra time and attention, but the constant demands of the infant invariably took precedence.

Nicholas was at a loss. He was useless at teaching them Palliteeler customs, and they had little time for him unless it was to listen to the ticking of his father's gold fob watch or examine the scrimshaw whale's tooth, both of which hung around his neck. The likeness of Nicholas etched into its surface never failed to fascinate, as it did the rest of the band. Initially the elders thought such a thing would surely bring evil spirits, but when nothing untoward happened, they gradually became accustomed to it, some even deciding it brought good luck.

Young men looked forward to the coastal meetings for reasons other than food, for such gatherings were an excellent opportunity to perhaps procure a mate from a neighbouring band. Much speculation occurred as the parents of eligible children examined likely candidates from other bands. Despite marrying couples having very little say about the partner chosen for them, rarely did the children disagree or protest the selection, such was their respect for parental decision. This season two new girls of about fourteen years of age were given to Pallitteeler youths and one Pallitteeler girl left to become the wife of a Norrettorre man. The occasion gave rise to night-long celebrations in the form of song and dance around the campfires.

In the summer, the band moved inland, resuming the age-old migratory pattern observed by the Pallitteeler in their continual quest for food.

Usually the change of season brought numerous encounters with kangaroos, but for reasons unknown to the hunters their numbers were greatly reduced that year, forcing the band to exist on smaller animals. Many older members succumbed to the harsh conditions, and morale among the remainder was low. By the time winter again turned to spring, they were bordering on starvation. Reprieve came with the water bird season at the coast, where once again they relished its rich bounty and, as other northern bands arrived, enjoyed the social interaction the gathering offered. It was the perfect climate for their spirits and bodies to heal.

By this time Buck was nearing his second birthday and Lucas his first. In appearance, the two boys were worlds apart, one a blue-eyed blond, the other inheriting a combination of his parents' features that produced deep, honey-coloured hair and caramel skin offset by his mother's dark, doe-like eyes. Yet during the height of summer, Buck's skin tone deepened to a colour only marginally lighter than his brother's. In personality, the boys were similar, both outgoing and curious about everything, and Nicholas adored them both, but while he outwardly appeared content with his new life and family, he was restless and disillusioned, craving the rudiments of a more familiar civilisation and the sound of his own language.

At first he thought the homesickness would pass, but time only made it worse. It made no sense, especially as he had been made so welcome. The gap between their two cultures should have diminished, but the longer he remained with the Pallitteeler and they seemingly began to know each other, the deeper the chasm somehow grew. It was something intangible—something he couldn't define—and eventually it became clear the gap could never be bridged and they would never fully understand one and other. Despite the outward friendliness, there remained an unspoken element of uncertainty, almost apprehension, on both sides. In a strange way, he now loved them all, would protect them with his life if it came to that, but at the same time, he yearned for the company of another European.

At these times, the indescribable gap seemed too immense.

Chapter 34

After considerable thought and weighing up of options Nicholas eventually decided he needed to return to white civilisation and accept whatever punishment was meted out. Of course, he could stay right where he was and quite probably have a very nice life, but it was just not the life he wanted. He needed a different kind of fulfilment, one with his own kind, his own culture. There was no denying he was giving up a lot and would cause pain, both to himself and Skyla, but he knew he simply couldn't continue with things as they were, and regardless of the outcome, he must risk facing the consequences of his actions to be with his own kind.

When Nicholas announced his plans to the band, everyone was shocked, some even angered, and many did their utmost to dissuade him, especially Skyla, but it was to no avail. His mind was made up.

From the beginning Nicholas planned to take Buck with him, but he changed his mind after realising the boy was unlikely to survive the long trip south to Hobart Town. He would be best left with the band. Tribal life was the only existence the boy knew, and it would be unfair to wrench him from all he loved and the only mother he had ever known and take him to a life he would probably hate. Even if the child survived the trip, what would await him? He'd be homeless when his father was arrested for desertion.

Pulled in two directions by logic and his love for the boy, Nicholas was tormented, but he saw no other way.

Taking Lucas was entirely out of the question, not only because of his tender age, but the fact that the band was not likely to give its consent. They considered both boys, but particularly Lucas, to be Pallitteeler, and every band member was needed and valued. Neither would be surrendered lightly.

The anguish of leaving his sons behind caused Nicholas to delay his departure, and in the end, he could only go by convincing himself he would someday return. He said goodbye to Buck first. Around the boy's neck he placed the gold chain and fob watch, into which he painstakingly had scratched his own name under that of his father, Lucas William Thomas, with the tip of his knife. He then etched the names *Margaret McKinnon, Buck William Thomas (1804) and Lucas (1805)* beneath his own. It was the only heritage he had to offer the lad.

Buck was far too young to understand what was happening, but was nevertheless delighted to receive a token of such importance and revelled in the fuss everyone made of him as he ran about in the morning sunshine gleefully displaying the glittering gift.

Nicholas then turned to Lucas who, not to be outdone, received his father's prized whale's tooth to hang about his neck, but not before Nicholas again took his knife and carved the name *Skylamahana* along with Buck and Lucas and the years of their birth. The English words would probably never mean anything to the lad, Nicholas lamented, but again, he had nothing else to leave him.

All morning Skyla remained pensive, not really believing Nicholas would leave, rationalising that leaving his sons would prove too painful, but when it became obvious he was ready to go, her composure dissolved. She threw her arms around his neck and pleaded for him to stay, but even her distraught tears failed to break his resolve, and embarrassed by the display, he firmly but gently took hold of her arms and pulled free.

"I must," he said, sidestepping her reach. Then in a vain attempt at reassurance, added, "But I will return."

To this she became hysterical. "Not get back," she cried, tears streaming down her face as she tried again to grab him. "I need you . . . boys need you."

Buck stared in wide-eyed confusion, tears brimming, then ran to his weeping mother's side. In the background, Lucas began to wail.

"Please! Not go," Skyla begged, sinking to her knees in the soft, loose dirt, searching for words to make him change his mind.

"I must go," Nicholas repeated, with rent heart and hollow stomach. The sooner he was gone, the better. Long goodbyes were agony for everyone. He took one long, last look at his family and turned and strode decisively from the camp.

Skyla ran after him, still pleading, but Nicholas didn't even turn around, for to do so would be his undoing, and when he heard Buck echoing his mother's words, he felt a pain in his chest like his heart was being crushed. With supreme effort, he increased his pace, knowing if he stopped now he would never leave. He then broke into a run, trying not to listen, and eventually the crying and pleading gave way to the sounds of the bush and a twiggy groundcover cracking under foot. He was alone, miles from the camp. Only then did he allow his emotions to surface. Blinded by tears, he stumbled, sobbing as he had not done since Maggie's death—but push on he must, because it would be an easy thing to return to the Pallitteeler as his heart now demanded. At this point Nicholas could almost forget the part of his soul that longed for European contact. Was he crazy to throw away what he had with the band to endure the journey south with all its dangers just to be with his own kind?

Were they still his kind?

Nicholas had no answer.

Driven by a force unknown, he was compelled to return to Hobart Town even if it meant ultimately being tried for desertion and possibly even shot.

Chapter 35

Winter was hard for Skyla and her children. The band generously gave them food, but it was customary for a man to provide for his family by joining the hunt, so she felt embarrassed and resentful of her situation when food was apportioned. Thus she resolved to find a husband at the next gathering on the coast and eagerly awaited the arrival of other bands.

But Skyla had not taken into account that few men were willing to take on a ready-made family as large as hers—three sons and a daughter—especially if two of the boys were of European descent. She was also much older than the normal marrying age, and with the prospective husbands being several years younger, they all sought young brides. Negotiations with their parents were unsuccessful. Even the representations of Warcottewilda led to nothing. A widower named Sulyukenny from the Plaihekehillerplue band was the right age, but he refused to take on the white children following unpleasant experiences with the western sealers, which included the kidnapping of his sister. He wanted nothing to do with the offspring of a white man. For him, it was entirely out of the question.

"The boys are white and will always be white," Sulyukenny said vehemently. "They might be young now, but it is within them to be cruel and murderous like the rest of their kind."

For days the man's words rang in Skyla's head, but there could be no truth in them. How could her gentle, lovable boys ever be like those sealers? It was impossible. Certainly their father was different, but like it or not, it was apparent these boys might never be fully accepted by another band, and while she had them, she too would never be accepted, would never find a husband. The more she dwelt on the problem, the clearer a solution became. The boys might be better off in European society, even Lucas, the child of her own body. At this point nausea always put an end to such thoughts, but she knew eventually it must be faced.

Warcottewilda was in total agreement. The differences between the two cultures were likely to get worse rather than better. Even Manekedru agreed it would be in everyone's best interest, particularly Buck's, to return them to the whites.

One full season had passed since Nicholas' departure, and no one thought it likely he would return, so they made the decision in his absence. Little Lucas, although lighter in hair and skin colour than the rest of the tribe, could probably blend in as Pallitteeler in later life, but would never be accepted by Sulyukenny and many of the Plaihekehillerplue, who would never marry Skyla while Lucas remained with her.

There was no question about Buck. He was white and must be returned to his own kind.

Discussions lasted for several days and, in the end, Manekedru, as leader of the Pallitteeler, decided both boys would be returned to white society. Skyla was told to take them to one of the sealer's settlements. Upon her return, she would be accepted by Sulyukenny.

Faced with their decision Skyla's first reaction was to argue, thinking she could fend for herself like she had over the past months and somehow scrape out a living sufficient enough to allow her to keep the boys. How could she ever let them go? They were both her children, and she loved neither one more than the other. It certainly was no fault of theirs that their father was white.

But it was no use. Try as she might, Skyla found no solution. It was impossible to keep the children and still get a husband. Common sense dictated that her own survival and that of the older children ultimately depended on her having a husband. Since she could not have both, she had no choice in the matter.

"There will be other children," Warcottewilda reassured. "And you still have your two eldest."

He was right, Skyla agreed, but it annoyed her that the two older children seemed pleased their younger siblings were about to leave forever, and only the emptiness of her loss and the energy it drained prevented her from delving deeper into their feelings. Instead, she consoled herself by acknowledging that rivalry existed between the children of both her families from almost the moment Nicholas and Buck arrived some three seasons ago—a long time. Perhaps they had never really been happy since then. Depleted of will, she could do little but be thankful they felt nothing of the pain she now endured.

The band's decision was shattering, but accept it she must, there was no question. It was made in everyone's best interest. Nevertheless, there were times when she considered the possibility of staying on with the sealers just to be with her children. It was only the fear of being harmed or forced into slavery that caused her to abandon such notions.

Despite all logic and reasoning, on the boys' last night, Skyla wished for death, wished she had never met Nicholas, wished there were no children, wished everything was different, but when her eyes opened in the morning, nothing had changed. She hardly noticed the bright, clear sky as she left the tribe to journey west along the coast with Buck toddling alongside and Lucas on her hip. Had there been an alternative solution, she would have taken it, anything rather than make this trip, but there was nothing, and her pace was not so much hampered by the children, but by the weight of her gloom.

After three days they came to a hut, its campfire cold. It was a barren place with nothing to indicate anyone had been there for several days, perhaps even weeks, and having no desire to wait and see if anyone returned, she continued west.

They smelled it long before the settlement came into view, its thick smoke and cloying, sweet odour wrinkling their nostrils. Skyla approached cautiously, her heart hammering as she settled into grassy concealment and stared at the bizarre sight. It was a dwelling such as she had never seen. Inside an enclosure made of wood slabs stood a huge, square structure fashioned from similar material, its sloping roof consisting of overlayed slabs of bark. At one end rose an enormous stone funnel, through which smoke billowed. Tales of these strange boxes were numerous, and Skyla had assumed she would be prepared, but when part of the wall opened and out stepped a woman clad in a long skirt similar to that worn by Nicholas' first woman, she was astonished beyond belief. Skyla clutched the children, trying to still her racing heart.

Only curiosity and the wriggling bodies on either side caused her to peek again. Buck's eyes were bulging, and Skyla quickly shushed him when he began to point and squeal. Lucas bit his bottom lip, his eyes showing an enormous amount of white. The woman carried a container of wet things similar to what she was wearing and proceeded to hang them on a rope strung between two poles. From the number of items, it was clear several people lived there, mostly men, judging by the row of grey britches similar to the white ones worn by Nicholas.

When the woman retreated inside, Skyla satisfied herself there were no men about at the moment, slipped inside the enclosure and started to circle the hut, which was situated back from the rocky beach in a sheltered clearing amongst the trees. As she did so, she discovered a second hut, then a third. If the boys had to be left anywhere, this was probably the best place. At least there was a woman to care for them. But what if she refused to take them? Half of her wanted the woman to decline so she could keep them a little longer while the other half of her panicked at the thought.

Skyla took each child firmly by the hand and marched back toward the first hut. The need to live with the whites had been explained to both boys along the way, even though Skyla knew they were far too young to fully comprehend. Despite Buck's reassurance of their bravery, how they would react to her final goodbye, she could not bear to contemplate. Best to get it over with quickly.

"Ullo," Skyla called out in the language Nicholas had spent so much time trying to teach her. When there was no reply, Skyla called again louder, "Ullooo." This time there was movement behind a small cut-out in the wall off to the side of the door before the woman again appeared at the door, a rifle in her hand.

"What d'ya want?" the woman answered, suspiciously.

"Children," Skyla said as calmly as her turmoil allowed. Slowly she moved closer, having enormous respect for the gun pointing in her direction. "You have children." A hand at Buck's back guided him forward, allowing the woman a clear view of the white child.

"You alone?" she asked, her eyes scanning the bush beyond the fence.

Skyla didn't understand, but recognised the woman's fear. "You take children," she repeated, ignoring the concern.

The two women stared at each other for a moment then the woman stepped from the doorway and approached the visitors, staring all the while at Buck before bending to inspect him more closely. As she did so, he reached out to touch her fair hair. It was similar to his own, just a few shades darker. From somewhere he remembered blue eyes like the ones now studying him, but the memory was a blur.

"What's ya name, child?" she grinned, revealing a row of faintly yellowed teeth. The boy drew back, not understanding her words.

Skyla resisted the urge to grab both children and run. "Him Buck Thomas," she said solemnly, opening the fob watch hanging from the boy's neck, indicating the woman read. "Father . . . Nicholas Thomas."

"I don't read words," the woman snapped. "Where'd ya find him?"

After several attempts at trying to make the woman understand their circumstances, Skyla's shoulders drooped and she shuffled her feet in the dirt, shaking her head while she searched for words. Exasperated, the woman called out to someone in the far hut, and to Skyla's astonishment, an aboriginal woman in European clothing came forth.

The woman answered to the name Bess, and because she was from the North-West tribe, Skyla was able to communicate every detail concerning Buck's and Lucas' parentage and why she could no longer keep them. Bess then translated for the blond woman, Eliza Harris, who made her reluctance to take Lucas clear by pushing him back towards Skyla, saying, "He's more black than white."

"No, he half-n-half," Bess stressed. "Band no want . . . has to stay here."

Skyla watched, bewildered, as the white woman continued to shake her head, and again she fought the urge to grab the boys and run. Instead, she placed Luke's hand in Buck's and nudged them forward while the women bantered back and forth, their voices becoming raised. Buck turned back, wide-eyed and questioning, and Skyla motioned him on despite his fear. In the end, Bess proposed that she would take care of Lucas if Mrs. Harris accepted Buck. Eliza Harris agreed.

Buck was able to stay brave until the moment of Skyla's hurried goodbye, and as she fled from the enclosure, both children screamed and clawed against restraining hands. They watched with disbelief as she vanished into the thick, green scrub. In the ensuing moments, Buck cried himself hoarse and refused to have anything to do with Mrs. Harris, seeking the familiar comfort of Bess' dark-skinned embrace and familiar language.

Skyla, far from impervious to the grief of her sons, raced headlong into the trees trying to block out their wailing, weaving this way and that, scrambling and stumbling as though pursued by something unseen, as if in fleeing she could outrun the demon. Vainly she tried to reassure herself that she had done the right thing, knowing nothing would ever deaden her agony. On and on she fled, stopping when several miles away, and then only to gulp a few rasping breaths before sprinting off again, for the clutch of the demon was ever present no matter how fast she ran, and the torture refused to abate. Still she ran on.

It was not quite dark when, utterly exhausted, Skyla fell to the ground in sheer misery and crawled under a clump of ferns protruding from the side of a disintegrating log, where she lay shaking with only her own arms for comfort.

Chapter 36

Lucas and Buck remained at the sealers' settlement under the care of Bess, the aboriginal woman of Ezra Ford, and visited Mrs. Harris' hut each afternoon for their English lessons. No one in camp could read or write, but at least learning to speak the language was a start. Because she made a game of it, the boys had no difficulty, quickly understanding the stories and rhymes she recited and eagerly awaiting the end of the lesson when they were permitted to examine the illustrations in old newspapers and the tattered old bible belonging to her husband Jeremiah.

They were fast learners and, by the summer of 1810, were fluent in their new language. When not playing on the beach, their favourite pastime was listening to Bess' aboriginal stories. She was determined the boys would retain something of their roots. The children clung to every word. The best stories, to the boys, were those about their father, the white man called Nicholas Thomas, and how he appeared in the bush with the woman who died giving birth to Buck before joining the Pallitteeler, teaching them about fire and becoming a hero. In time he married the beautiful Skylamahana, who bore him

Lucas then returned to his own people camped on a river far to the south.

Of course Bess embellished the story for the boys, making up minor details to cover the gaps in her knowledge, but always keeping the essential elements unchanged. Inevitably, their father attained superhuman status in their minds. He was the mighty warrior who brought fire to the people who had none. Papa Thomas, as they referred to him, was someone they could be proud of.

While the women saw to many aspects of the boys' education, the sealers taught them about tools, weapons, and the habits of seals. Many a promise had been made to take them out sealing when they were old enough. Buck, who already exhibited an excellent aim with a harpoon, could hardly wait for the day, convinced he would be the greatest hunter of all. Lucas naturally thought he would be best and tried to match his older brother in every aspect. The two were good companions, spending many happy hours playing along the shore, exploring rock pools, and pretending to be hunters.

In early 1811, the boys' morning game among the rocks to the west of the settlement was interrupted by the passing of a large ship, which curiously altered course, sailed toward them, and dropped anchor several hundred yards off shore. When a small boat was lowered and three men began rowing toward the settlement, Buck and Lucas raced back along the beach to break the news. Few ships called in those days. The north coast was all but hunted out, so any ship was cause for great excitement.

A group from the settlement greeted the men as the boat

pulled into the shallows. The three on board splashed into the water and hauled the craft onto the sand. Two white men greeted the group while the other, a tall black man, darker than anyone the boys had ever seen, threw the anchor onto dry sand. In a matter of minutes, it was established they were not there for sealing. The ship was an American whaler in need of fresh water before heading back to the Pacific Ocean. When the settlement was sighted, they assumed there must be a good supply of water nearby.

"There's a stream to the west, just beyond the rocks," Jeremiah pointed. "But surely you'll stay the night? We can use the company and news from outside."

"No, we must be on our way, although it's good to stand on dry ground again," the first man said with a laugh. "Capn's a waiting. Gave us orders to fill these kegs and get back for the next lot, so we'd best be moving."

"Then we'll give you a hand," replied Jeremiah, glancing at Ezra, who nodded his agreement.

"Me too," chimed Buck, skipping off in the direction from which he had just come, Lucas bouncing along behind.

The black man's eyes fixed on the younger boy with the whale's tooth dangling from his neck and his mind raced back to 1803. How was it possible? With large strides, he caught up to the trailing boy. "What's ya name, boy?"

"Lucas," he replied, matter-of-factly, slowing down. "What's yours?"

"They calls me Big Buck Jones."

"My brother's called Buck."

"That so?" Big Buck glanced ahead at the blond boy. "That him?"

Lucas nodded, breaking into a trot. "Hey, Buck, wait up."

"What's that ya got round ya neck?"

"It's mine." Lucas clutched the tooth and darted sideways.

"I ain't got no mind to take it, boy. I's just curious."

Lucas turned warily before being taken in by the big man's broad, white grin. "It's special, left by my father for me," Lucas replied, holding up the tooth, its cord still around his neck. "He was a brave warrior. This is him here, see?"

Big Buck bent over, took the tooth into his hand and rolled it over, instantly recognised it as the one he carved for Nicholas all those years ago. "I used ta know ya father . . . he was a good man," he said, pensively. "I bet ya doesn't know I carved this here tooth for him."

The boys stared at the tall black man, disbelief furrowing lines across their brows. "No you didn't," retorted Lucas, unsure whether he should be angry or laugh at the preposterous joke.

"It's true," the big man insisted. "See, this be me on the back." Buck turned the tooth over to show the boy, but was met with a blank stare. "Guess I looks a might older now," he chuckled, before releasing the tooth and standing to full height. "Used ta do a lot of that back then . . . me eyes ain't so good now."

"Our father was Nicholas Thomas," Buck said, suspiciously. "He was a Pallitteeler hero. How could you have known him?"

"I knowed him long afore then, when he was a soldier. We met on the ship that brung him here."

Jeremiah Harris caught up. "Their father was a soldier?"

"Yassir, one of the New South Wales Corps. He was with Bowen's party . . . came ta settle Van Diemen's Land. The whaler I was on got commissioned for the voyage. I never saw Nick agin after that, but we was good mates, that's for sure. I carved that as a partin' gift." Big Buck gestured toward the tooth. "Never thought ta see it on his son. Is Nick living here?"

"Nah, no one knows what happened to him. My guess is he's probably dead."

Little effort was required for Big Buck to convince the sealers they should return young Buck Thomas to Hobart Town. If Nicholas Thomas was still alive and could be located, it was right that his son be returned to him and, although Bess objected, clutching the boy to her ample breast, the others saw merit in the idea. So as the western sun dipped toward the horizon, young Buck found himself beside the tall black American on the deck of the whaler watching his home on the coast recede. Only the hope of being reunited with his father kept the tears at bay. Big Buck said he would find him, and the boy had no cause to doubt, but the big man acknowledged only to himself that it mightn't be possible. In any event, he wanted the best for the lad. If his father couldn't be found, he would find a good home for the boy, one where he would be educated and given the opportunity to make something of himself.

Much discussion over Lucas' future had taken place, but the colour of his skin told everyone he would stand little chance of acceptance in Hobart Town and would be far better off staying with Bess and learning the sealing trade. Lucas desired nothing more than to be a grownup sealer, but when it came to being separated from his brother, that was quite something else, and when bellowing his protests failed to sway the adults' decision, he flew at Big Buck, thumping small fists into his muscled thigh. The big man scooped up the struggling child, who was well beyond reasoning with, and vainly tried to quell his fury before a resolute Bess whisked him away. Big Buck considered the possibility of taking him to his own family in America, a stupid idea he quickly dismissed.

As it turned out, the ship's captain would have none of any of it. Children were bad luck. Only grudgingly did he agree to just one child on board, and then for only a few days at the most; taking two children was quite out of the question. Bent on keeping to his timetable, the captain then refused to re-route their voyage to visit Hobart Town, his only concession being a minor detour to the new northern township at Port Dalrymple, only a day's sail east along the coast. Here young Buck was to be deposited.

Meanwhile a marvellous adventure was unfolding for little Buck, who in his excitement, shed few tears and appeared impervious to the inconsolable Lucas. All explanations were useless to him, and the child shrieked and struggled to follow his brother into the dingy. Breaking free of Bess' grasp, he splashed into the waves after the heavily laden craft screaming at the top of his lungs. "Bucky, Bucky. Wait for me. I'm coming with you."

The oarsmen propelled the boat swiftly past the breakers beyond his grasp, but he continued to flounder towards them. Only when the clear, green water became too deep did the screams subside, and it was Bess who hauled the whimpering boy back to the shallows and safety.

Young Buck watched in stony silence, a prominent pout the sole evidence of a stoicism not yet mastered. From the mists of long ago, he recalled a similar reaction when together they screamed for Skyla, but such memories were blurred by time, and he knew Lucas had no similar recollection. He was too small at the time . . . he was still too small. His brother was made to stay behind because he was too young for such a voyage, or so he was told. When he was older, he could come to Hobart Town.

"I'll be waiting there for you," Buck promised the sobbing Lucas just before he left. And it was a vow he was absolutely positive he would keep.

He watched the settlement until it was almost out of sight, waving occasionally, before turning his attention to the gently creaking ship as she was propelled through the swell by taut canvas overhead. Waves looked different from this new perspective, where the ocean was bottomless, and even the foam formed unfamiliar patterns as the bow sliced across the blue-green depths.

Everywhere there was something new and exciting to examine. And examine everything, he did, from bow to stern then bulwark to bulwark. Then he was taken below deck, where the sleeping arrangements were explained and he was instructed to keep well away from the captain, especially his cabin at the end of the dark corridor. The tour ended in the galley, where a supper of stew and biscuit was eaten with several men before he retired to listen to Big Buck's tales of his father and their voyage from Sydney Town to Van Diemen's Land. Lulled by the motion of the ship, he soon fell asleep on the makeshift, yet comfortable, pallet of blankets made for him in a corner of the bunk room.

In the morning, the ship tacked smoothly into Port Dalrymple, silently rippling the almost perfect reflection of the tree-lined riverbank as they passed up the Tamar, a wide, deep river named after the one flowing through Launceston in Cornwall, the birthplace of Governor King. In keeping with this tradition, a small village nestling several miles upstream from their destination of George Town was now known as Launceston.

The penal settlement of George Town on the eastern shore was a fine-looking community founded six years earlier by Lieutenant Colonel William Patterson who, as a captain in the New South Wales Corps, arrived in Sydney Town in 1791 and rapidly progressed to being governor of Norfolk Island then Sydney Town.

George Town, still essentially a penal settlement, was a closed port, so the whaler remained well offshore, anchoring closer to the western bank, after which word was sent to Major Gordon, the commanding officer of Port Dalrymple. Several hours passed during which the plight of young Buck Thomas was explained through a relay of boat trips before he and Big Buck were permitted ashore under soldier escort.

There were some thirteen hundred people in and around Port Dalrymple, and Buck had never seen so many buildings or people. His eyes grew rounder by the minute. He knew all about soldiers with their swords and shiny boots, towns with their horse-drawn wagons, and houses with two storeys—Eliza Harris had seen to that—but their reality filled him with awe. The horses were altogether astonishing; she'd said they were big, with people riding on their backs, yet he never imagined them as enormous as the one hauling the wagonload of wood that caused them to pull up short as it rattled across their path.

Their escort, a soldier from the seventy-third regiment, led them past the clanking furnace of the blacksmith's workshop with its acrid smell and round the corner toward a solid stone building, the headquarters of Major Gordon. Here they would decide the future of young Buck Thomas.

Chapter 37

James McCabe, a Norfolk Island evacuee, arrived in Van Diemen's Land with his wife Ann and nine-year-old twins, Richard and Rebecca. James was a strong, active man of forty-two years who, as a marine, set sail for Botany Bay with the first fleet in 1787, but soon after arrival was sent with Lieutenant Philip Gidley King's contingent to Norfolk Island to claim it for Britain before the French established a foothold. The French had visited the island shortly before the first fleet arrived, but were unable to land due to the combination of a rugged coastline, rough seas, and high winds. King's party encountered better conditions.

King was accompanied by a mere twenty-two people aboard the *Supply*, consisting of convicts and marines. The party arrived in mid-February after two weeks at sea to discover the island was almost totally covered by tall pine trees and a thick tangle of vines, the likes of which they had never seen before. They immediately set to work clearing the area opposite Sydney Bay, named after the new settlement in New South Wales, and a storehouse and a few dwellings were soon erected using the soft, straight pine wood that was so abundant. Gardens were quickly established in the temperate climate and the settlement prospered, King was made commandant then later, lieutenant governor, and their numbers grew with the arrival of seven more marines and thirty-two convicts the following October. Shiploads of convicts to the island continued, and four years later, it boasted a population of over one thousand people.

By this time, James McCabe had completed his marine service and decided to settle on the island. Ex-service settlers were entitled to land grants of sixty acres. James' selection was located in the area known as Charlotte's Field, to the west of Mount Pitt, which at one thousand and thirty-eight feet, was the highest point on Norfolk Island. As well as receiving land, he was provided with free tools, two breeding sows, six hens, and provisions from the government store. To enable him to clear half an acre of land and build a hut, two convicts were also assigned to him for the first nine weeks.

But these allowances were not provided by the government free of restriction. Free settlers had to become independent of the public store within eighteen months, support a woman who must be off the public store within twelve months, and the following year provide for one male convict off the public store. Such measures were essential to ensure the settlement became self-sufficient and prosperous instead of relying on government store handouts.

Like most of the settlers in Charlotte's Field, James' acres grew a variety of vegetables as well as quantities of wheat and Indian corn. Because the island's soil was rich to a minimum depth of nine inches, most crops produced a good return with much of the island's produce, particularly in the early days, shipped to Sydney Town. James was more fortunate than many other settlers, his land being largely arable, whereas some selected steep undulating land that made reaping a profit difficult and sometimes impossible.

The only fault with James' grant was a tract of marshy land adjacent to the creek. Undaunted, he set about encouraging the growth of the island's natural flax plant in this area, aware that the harvesting of flax had been supported by the government from the moment of colonisation and his scheme could prove very profitable.

Because New Zealand was producing luxuriant flax products, the lieutenant governor looked in that direction for advice on local flax production. When the Maori consultants arrived, they made suggestions as to how to improve the processing of the native flax, and soon the island was producing canvas of sail-making quality as well as clothing, but James' attempt to cultivate the local product was only marginally successful. Although the cultivated crop grew well, it turned out to be no better than the wild-grown crop, and in view of its labour intensity, James concluded it was not a profitable venture and ceased cultivation, as did many other experimenters. Wild flax continued to be processed, but James concentrated on his proven crops, and within a few years, he was one of the more prosperous settlers of Norfolk Island.

Yet in producing a family, James was not so prosperous. The woman he chose was Ann Frost, a convict from London with flashing, brown eyes and auburn hair, who arrived in 1789. Instantly attracted, James worked at establishing a relationship, something she willingly allowed herself to fall into, as was customary on the island. Even Lieutenant Governor King partook of a relationship with a convict woman that produced five children, all born on the island. Nevertheless, promotion of the family unit was emphasised, and lewd or lecherous behaviour frowned upon; hence, James McCabe took Ann Frost to be his woman and later his lawful wife. Ann proved to have difficulty carrying a child to term, being plagued by miscarriages or stillbirths, and it was not until 1799 that the couple successfully reproduced, when as though to make up for lost time, twins were born: a boy and a girl, whom they named Richard and Rebecca. Following their birth, Ann continued to have miscarriages, and it became apparent there would be no more children.

The McCabe family grew comfortably into their prosperity. Although the work was often hard, the rewards were great. They always had ample food on the table, were always well clothed, and James was even able to extend their small house by an additional two rooms, also installing a few modern conveniences. It was little wonder then, when the first rumours of the island's evacuations started, James was gravely concerned. The rumours turned out to be true, and it seemed all his hard work had gone for nothing.

Correspondence went back and forth for months, but the island's Lieutenant Governor Joseph Foveaux officially broke the news in 1803. It seemed Governor King, now in New South Wales, had spoken well of the island and managed to delay a decision for a time; nevertheless, the British government ultimately decided to abandon the island. The reasons given were its lack of safe anchorage, its distance from the mainland, and the resultant expense in its upkeep.

When Foveaux announced that most of the population was to be evacuated to Van Diemen's Land, the settlers were up in arms—none the least, James—but there was nothing to be done. Determined to abandon the island, the government offered whatever it took to gain settler cooperation, including a double land grant in Van Diemen's Land free of any conditions in replacement of the land lost, cattle, and as new settlers, rations from the government store. Most Norfolk Islanders bewailed the fact that such a move necessitated starting all over again . . . building . . . tilling the soil, but their protests came to naught.

Prudently, the government allowed them plenty of time to adjust to the idea, with the first departure of thirty-four settlers not occurring until November of 1807. Three additional parties set sail for the Derwent before the McCabe family boarded the *City of Edinburgh* in September the following year. This ship carried the largest contingent of Norfolk Islanders to Hobart Town: two hundred and forty-two people in all. What was planned to be an uneventful voyage was disrupted when the vessel was blown out to sea during a gale before it was fully loaded. For two weeks, she was buffeted by the storm before limping back to the island for repairs, after which she finally set sail for Van Diemen's Land. Fifteen hundred miles later, the *City of Edinburgh* at last dropped its anchor off Hobart Town. It was the first week in October 1808.

"Oh, it's a beautiful township," Ann said of the riverside settlement snuggled at the base of the magnificent Mount Wellington. She squeezed her husband's arm, and James felt her excited skip as they jostled for a better view amid the crowd by the bulwark. "It's a wonderful place to start a new life."

"It's certainly very different to our island," James said, stepping aside so the twins could see. "That, I'll grant you."

At their first glimpse of Cape Raol and Adventure Bay, it seemed their new home was little different to Norfolk Island with its hostile cliffs, but further into the bay, they saw jagged walls gave way to green hills. "Perhaps this place will be better," a few of the doubters conceded, but many stuck to the belief that nothing could replace the hard-won and much loved farms they'd left behind. Nevertheless, as the ship approached the Derwent, the entire deck became a mass of pushing passengers all craning their necks when it became apparent the rolling hills were punctuated by broad, lush meadows.

"I've never seen so many big buildings," squealed Rebecca, her nose just above the railing.

"Me neither," said Richard, clambering for a better view until he was supported by his stomach on the rail. "Look at that one on the hill."

"Get down, Son. It's dangerous." his mother warned, as James grabbed Richard by the belt and hauled him back until the boy's feet found the deck.

"Aw, Papa, I was only looking."

"You'll see it all soon enough. We'll be disembarking shortly. Take your sister's hand and stay nearby."

It was well past midday when the Norfolk Islanders began to spill onto the wharf and mill about, waiting for their possessions to be off loaded. Quickly bored by yet another hold-up, a group of children began to amuse themselves with a game of hide and seek among the piles of cargo and crates off to the side.

"Can we join in, Mama?" Richard asked, already tugging Rebecca along. Ann deferred to her husband, and Richard, recognising his father's hesitation, added, "Pleeease."

When Rebecca echoed her brother's plea, James found himself nodding. "But don't go near the water," he called, as the pair ran off.

A multitude of bags and boxes from the *City of Edinburgh* soon added colour to the mass of raw timber crates on the wharf. There was little order to the proceedings as families grappled for their own items amid the growing conglomerate, and no one paid heed to the repeated shifting levels of baggage or an occasional tumbling crate. It had been a long day, and with the sun getting lower, all they wanted was to find their belongings and get settled for the evening.

Surrounded by several bags, James and Ann were still hunting for the rest when Rebecca returned, taking her mother's hand. "Richard's found a good hiding place because no one can find him," she smiled proudly.

Ann looked to the group of returning children whose game was now breaking up, and scanned the faces for Richard. "You were supposed to stay together," she said, an accusing tone clipping her words as she sensed something very wrong.

Rebecca's smile vanished. "He wouldn't stay with me . . . said he wanted to hide by himself because I giggle too much and give the hiding spot away."

Ann sighed, knowing it was exactly the attitude her wilful and competitive son would have expressed. "Show me where you last saw him," she said, hurrying down the wharf.

With her daughter in tow, Ann searched in the vicinity of the rows of crates both on and off the wharf as well as the timber storehouses, where it seemed she found a myriad of nooks in which a small boy could hide, but none that held her son. Frustrated, Ann returned to her husband with a growing sense of alarm.

"He didn't even answer my calls," she told him, tears blurring her vision.

"Perhaps the boy's fallen into the water," a nearby eavesdropper suggested.

All unloading activities were suspended while James and the remaining men, perhaps forty in number, leapt into the murky depths in search of young Richard. For more than an hour, they continued to dive, probing the bottom in every possible location from the wharf's end to the shoreline and back again without success.

Fatigued and disheartened, the men slowly drifted away, returning one by one to their families and baggage while James, refuting exhaustion, continued diving in the area adjacent to the cargo crates, leaving Ann to pace the length of the wharf. Only when most of the boxes were claimed was the unconscious boy discovered pinned beneath one of the weighty wooden crates, which had crushed his lower limbs.

Chapter 38

The doctor's eyes were grave. "His shattered bones will probably heal in time," he informed James and Ann, who were now in dazed shock. "I've splinted both legs and his right arm, but I'm concerned about damage to the flesh of his legs."

"But there's hardly a scratch on him," James said, his words more a question than a statement.

"Quite right, there's very little in the way of visual marking. I'm concerned about the bruising, which I suspect will be significant following a crush like the lad's sustained," the doctor stated, then not wanting to alarm the family further, added, "What he needs now is rest. We'll keep him in the infirmary, and I'll see him again in the morning."

But the next day, Richard's legs had swollen to twice their normal size and had taken on a mottled, purplish tinge.

"If the boy survives the next week," the doctor informed his parents, "then he may pull through, but it's possible the crushing was so severe, he'll end up with kidney damage. I've seen it before when men get pinned under heavy weights. If this happens and his kidneys fail, then I'm afraid there'll be no hope for the lad."

"What causes the kidney damage?" James asked.

"We don't know," came the doctor's pensive reply. "My guess is it's something to do with squashed flesh and the body, including the kidneys, trying to heal itself. Perhaps they get overwhelmed."

"Can't you do something . . . anything?" Ann implored, her throat so constricted her words were just audible. "There must be some way to prevent it."

Ann's horrified gaze darted from the doctor to her husband and back again. She felt the pressure of James' hand on her arm and turned to see his eyes filled with hollow pain, and for the first time since the accident, she realised she was not alone in her anguish.

"I'm sorry," the doctor said, gathering his equipment. "Just keep him comfortable and pray." Ill at ease with their grief, he hastily left, leaving a resounding emptiness to replace the hope they had placed on him.

But pray they did, and forty-eight hours later, when Richard appeared to improve, even taking a little broth and bread, James and Ann thought their prayers had been answered. Most of the next few days were spent fussing over the boy and relaying exciting tales they had heard about the colony, but he remained listless, and neither parent was able to voice to the other their observation that their son's kidneys had ceased to function.

By the week's end, Richard's legs were a deep purple, and he lapsed into unconsciousness. Ann and James maintained a bedside vigil, trying to will him to live. Even Rebecca sat silently staring at her brother's increasingly ashen and bloated face, while both parents wondered if she, too, prayed or if she even fully understood the gravity of the situation. Neither were capable of extricating themselves from their own private sorrow to embrace the girl. It was the doctor who eventually ushered Rebecca away, entrusting her to the care of a nearby family.

Another week of silent torment passed, and at its close Richard McCabe, aged nine years of age, finally slipped from under the incessant prayers. The son they had so desperately wanted was lowered into the cool October earth of Hobart Town's cemetery, leaving his trembling, tormented parents wishing for death themselves, longing to be released from their agony and become as numb as they imagined his cold little body to be.

Chapter 39

Norfolk Islander families received land grants of between thirty and fifty acres in areas adjacent to Hobart Town, across the Derwent at Pittwater and at inland areas they'd named New Norfolk and Norfolk Plains, yet many immigrants failed to see the value in their new acquisitions. Others were disinclined to repeat the hard effort it takes to establish a new farm and, while still on public stores, bartered away their property for a few bottles of spirit.

"I can't understand them," James commented, shaking his head, and accepting the cool lemonade Ann brought out to the new fence, where her husband had been digging postholes since sun up. "It's like they've lost all will. Why can't they see the opportunities here?

Ann shrugged and topped up his glinting tin mug while he swiped sweat from his forehead with a dusty arm. "It's all too hard," she said. "And they can't be bothered."

"Yes, but even some who've put in the effort and get the soil tilled, like Dave Browning, still get despondent."

"I hear his land gave a poor yield," Ann said, sipping from

her own mug. "He's blaming it on poor quality soil and curses the day everyone was forced to leave the fertile farms of Norfolk Island."

"Well, I have to admit, this soil is very different, but our island days are over, and it will do none of us any good to whine over it," James said, in a tone revealing his exasperation. "What's done is done, and I, for one, don't intend to fail here."

"I know you don't," she murmured. "And nor do I." There was sadness in her voice as she added, "Life must go on."

James had heard those words many times over the past months and watched a steely determination set on Ann's face as she gathered her utensils, and James reached again for the crowbar.

"More lemonade before I start the washing?"

He shook his head. "If I keep going, I may finish this side by sundown." He watched her return to their two-room wooden dwelling, her once new lilac dress now tattered about the hem. Yes, they had both been shattered by the loss of their son, but they were still determined to make a good life for themselves and their daughter in Van Diemen's Land. It would have been easy to give up like so many others had it not been for their daughter. Young Rebecca's future depended on their efforts. She was their future too, and somehow this knowledge fuelled their motivation to work harder and more cleverly.

A little over twelve months ago, James had selected land at New Norfolk, where he and Ann energetically set to build a profitable farm with crops and cattle. Many sacrifices were made, and within the year, James was able to purchase an adjacent property from a disheartened Norfolk Islander. Currently he was negotiating the purchase of a further fifty acres at Norfolk Plains west of the Macquarie River in the mid-north of the island, and it looked as though three more families would also be selling out to him. Although part of him was angered by his former island neighbours' lack of stamina and will to persist, he was more than pleased with the opportunity to relieve them of the land they perceived so burdensome. At times he worried where the money was coming from, but inevitably any deficit was met by bartering, leaving both parties pleased with the deal.

By 1811 James McCabe was the owner of almost four hundred acres of land, one hundred at New Norfolk and the remainder in the north at Norfolk Plains, on which he grew crops and grazed cattle. The smaller property was now under the management of his bondservant, Billy Hargan, allowing James and his family, along with the cattle, to move north to Norfolk Plains. His plan was to continue growing wheat at New Norfolk while expanding its growth, but concentrate on the northern property by building up his stock of cattle. Hard work paid off. Both farms proved prosperous, and his small family wanted for nothing, every whim being fulfilled. But somewhere deep inside, James craved for what the farm could not produce: a son.

Instead, he focussed on Rebecca, who was shaping up to be a fine young lady, one who would have her choice of almost any young man she fancied, and if James had his way, she'd choose a wealthy farmer's son or an educated businessman from Hobart Town or Sydney. Either way, her future looked assured, yet still he craved a son, someone to be his heir and one day take over the management of the property he had worked on so hard. Someone he could guide and train in all matters of agriculture and business. It seemed a small thing to ask, but try as they might, Ann had moved beyond her years to conceive.

Outwardly, they appeared a happy couple, and in every

other aspect, they were. Neighbours and acquaintances never suspected the McCabe's extravagances were in some small way to compensate for their private sorrow. It was during the spring of 1812 that Ann insisted on a trip to George Town instead of the nearer Launceston. She wanted to make her purchases directly from the merchant before the goods reached the more expensive Launceston shopkeepers, where they usually sought their supplies.

"A penny saved is a penny invested," she liked to say.

As usual, James conceded, even though the village of Launceston, with its newer stores, was more convenient.

"Well, I'll be . . ." James exclaimed, placing his hand on his wife's, whose arm linked through his, as they negotiated the boardwalk along the shop front. "Isn't that Big Buck Jones? What's he doing in George Town?"

A disbelieving Ann blinked and focussed on the tall, dark frame lumbering towards them. They had met Big Buck briefly years ago when his ship anchored off Norfolk Island for supplies. "My goodness," she whispered. "It really is him."

"Good afternoon. Mr. Jones," James beamed, nodding to the seaman. "You're the last person we'd ever expect to see here."

Buck, standing a respectful distance from the well-dressed gentleman, who had taken him by complete surprise, ripped the hat from his head and bowed slightly to Ann. "Ya has the better of me, sir," he said, searching his memory.

"Norfolk Island," James prompted.

"Ah," Buck said, with a broad grin. "Mr. and Mrs. McCabe. Forgive me, I did na recognise you in your . . ." he hesitated to say finery. "It's been so long . . . years."

"That it has. What brings you to these parts?"

When the unfortunate circumstances of young Buck

Thomas, who had just a few moments ago been left with Major Gordon, were explained, Ann and James exchanged glances, each knowing what the other was thinking. Within the hour, Buck Thomas, son of a convict and a corps man, was adopted by James and Ann McCabe and henceforth known as Thomas "Buck" McCabe.

Chapter 40

Ezra Ford tightened his coat against the westerly wind and squinted into the rain. It hadn't let up all day, and he was returning home empty-handed again. Gone were the days of plenty. He was feeling the effects of over-harvesting and knew it would get harder and harder to make a living at sealing along the north coast, proving what he always knew: nothing lasts forever.

Through the grey, he could see a ship near the horizon heading east. It was not a whaler, but he assumed it had called at the camp for water as did so many others.

He rounded a rocky outcrop and all but fell over the slender, dark frame huddled behind it. Lucas was drenched to the skin, partly covered in sand and sobbing in a moment of childish weakness.

"What is it, laddie?" enquired Ezra, bending down to comfort the boy.

"The men from the ship . . . they called me a nigger," he wailed, seeking refuge in the warmth of Ezra's protective arms. "But you always said I'm just the same as they are on the inside. I am, aren't I?"

Ezra sighed. "Aye, that you are, laddie." It was not the first time he had been called to comfort the seven-year-old. It had all started after Buck's departure. The first months were the hardest when colic gripped his stomach and he would not be consoled. Ezra had let the boy go his own way in the hope he would find his own understanding. Acceptance came slowly, and he saw the agony that accompanied the boy's realisation that his age was not the reason that had stopped him from going with Buck; it was the colour of his skin. Having aboriginal blood in his veins was something Lucas would have to deal with many times over throughout his life. The pain, Ezra knew, would never abate, and he feared the same for his own children.

"All they s . . . s . . . see is my s . . . skin," Lucas shivered. "It's not fa . . . fair."

"T'aint nothin' in this world that's necessarily fair, laddie. You'd best get used to it. It'll not be going to change."

"Well, I don't want to be d . . . different. I hate it. And I wish I could w . . . w . . . wash it off like d . . . dirt."

Ezra remembered catching Lucas in the bath several times over the past years, scouring his soaped-up skin with a brush, almost to the point of making it bleed. He was sure the boy would have kept it up had not Bess confiscated the implement and ordered him from the tub.

Ezra scooped the boy into his arms. "Let's be off, now. It's time we were both home. A hot tub will do us both good, but it's pointless you scrubbing at yourself. Your God-given colour will never wash off, no matter how hard you try. When all's said and done, it's what's in a man's heart that counts, not the colour of his skin. And try as you may, you cannot change the way you are, boy. You'd do well to find a way of accepting it."

Life was good when there were no visitors to the camp. Lucas learned the habits of seals and the skills of sealing. He was a quick learner and displayed a unique understanding of the weather, the sea, and all wildlife. When one of their boats broke its mooring, it was Lucas' understanding of the local currents that led to the craft's location and the salvaging of several items from the nearby shallows.

Approaching his teens, Lucas' innate knowledge earned him the admiration and respect of men who had spent most of their lives sealing in the southern oceans. Lacking in physical strength only, his other skills soon matched the best of them. It was not long before he was accompanying the men on all their major ventures. In this he found fulfilment and a new drive to succeed. Before long he was entirely self-sufficient and, when left to his own devices, found peace and contentment in solitude.

Only the trickle of outside visitors caused him angst, the ones who regarded him with contempt, not even bothering to speak to him and taking their business directly to either Ezra or one of the other white sealers. It never occurred to him, since he was doing the work of a man, that any of them might consider him still a boy. In his younger years, the repeated reminders that he was different would send him into hiding until after the visitors had gone, but now he was simply fed up with being on the receiving end of so many down-the-nose stares and snide comments about being a half-breed. Lucas had learned to stand his ground and began challenging anyone who treated him in any way different.

Bess told him he was insolent and courting trouble, but undeterred, Lucas continued to give as good as he received. She learned to be ready for anything whenever there was company.

The sand was hot underfoot one morning in February as Lucas went down to greet another lot of newcomers. "State your business!" he shouted, always aware some visitors might be up to no good.

"We're in need of fresh water and meat if you have any," the red-shirted mariner said, as the group stepped from their beached dinghy. "Who's in charge here?"

"I'm in charge until the others return," Lucas replied. "There's plenty of water upstream." He pointed towards the trees where the little stream disappeared. "You're welcome to help yourselves, but the meat we usually sell or trade. How much do you need?"

"What would the likes of you know about selling anything?"

Lucas returned the man's icy gaze while his two companions sniggered. "I know enough about selling and trading to know you'll get nothing here unless you offer a fair price."

"We ain't doin' business with no black bastard."

"Then you'd better get your water and be on your way."

"This is a sealers' camp, right?"

Lucas nodded.

"When do the sealers get back?"

"I'm a sealer."

"You know what I mean, nigger-boy."

"In a week or two," Lucas lied, knowing they wouldn't wait that long for Ezra and the others to return. "So you'll have to deal with me if you want meat." His upper lip curled into a baiting sneer.

"We don't buy from blacks."

"And I don't deal with white scum," Lucas shot back. He turned his back, but stopped short at the sound of a pistol cocking. As he slowly turned to face the man and his weapon, from the corner of his eye he saw Bess and the other women and children dart into their huts. If necessary they could slip out the back into the trees, shielded from view by the slab structures. The gun the man brandished was like nothing Lucas had ever seen before and nothing like Ezra's old flintlock, and he assumed it was one of the new percussion-cap pistols he had heard about.

"We'll take whatever we damned well want from you blacks. Now go get that meat . . . all of it, mind you, before there's more of your blood on the sand than in your veins."

"I don't do business with the likes of you," Lucas repeated, trying to control the stammer creeping into his voice and wishing he had not lied about Ezra's late return. The fact was the others were only on a short supply trip to Launceston and due back the following evening. If these men thought their return was imminent, he was convinced they would think twice about their behaviour. "You'd best be on your way. Just get your water and go."

"Don't be telling us what to do, nigger." The man waved his pistol menacingly in front of Lucas' face. "Now get that meat."

Lucas didn't move.

"Well, hop to it, nigger, 'fore I scatter yer brains."

The boom of musket fire sent them all to sand.

"What the . . ." one of them cried, after Bess' bullet sailed overhead. Their bellies smacked the sand, and they floundered in the golden grit, frantically searching for the shooter. Only when they spotted her walking slowly towards them, her musket trained on the man with the pistol and her finger ready to squeeze, did they become motionless.

"I'd be dropping that hand piece if I were you," Lucas said, regaining his feet then adding sarcastically, "unless, of course, you want more of your brains out on the sand than in your skull."

"Tha's right, Mister," Bess said, stepping from grass to sand. "I's not too scared ta blow ya head off ya shoulders. And don't ya others move a whisker less ya want the cur as dead as I do."

Bess allowed Lucas to take control of the musket. He saw the man's fingers tighten around his pistol as he searched for an opportunity to use it. Lucas offered none, keeping the long barrel pointed firmly at the man's head.

"Toss the pistol here," Lucas demanded. When the man hesitated he added, "I won't ask you again."

Any fear the man felt was overshadowed by his hate, for that was all Lucas could see in the man's cold stare. Then, without a word, he succumbed.

Bess quickly retrieve the weapon from where it landed a few feet away.

"Now unload those two barrels, get your water, and be gone," Lucas commanded.

It was not until the trio's boat had passed the breakwater that Lucas and Bess lowered their weapons. "I hopes that's the last we seen o' them," Bess said. "No thanks to ya, either. Ya shouldn't be goadin' people like ya does. Damn near got ya head blown off this time."

"They deserved what they got," Lucas said, his eyes still flashing. "The bastards could have simply bought what they needed without throwing insults about. I wasn't looking for trouble. I wouldn't put it past them to come back tonight looking for more of it, so I'll keep watch to make sure they don't try anything."

Thankfully it was an uneventful, if sleepless, night.

Although he never welcomed visitors from passing ships, Lucas always looked forward to visits by aboriginal bands, but being unable to communicate beyond sign language, they had little in common. As their visits became less frequent, he tried even harder to establish a relationship, but the more he tried the less interest they displayed. Regardless of his colouring, he concluded that in their eyes he was white, and they had little use for Europeans beyond a little trade. Logic told him there was little hope, but his soul told him otherwise and, as the years passed, his hopes for aboriginal acceptance accelerated in proportion to his disappointment with Europeans. He always scanned their faces for some sign of acceptance or recognition that he was a part of them. He saw none. Lucas was excluded from both cultures.

Chapter 41

He was totally unaware of her silent approach as he went about the business of chopping then stacking fire wood against the side of the hut until the hairs on the back of his neck prickled with the eerie feeling of another human presence. Lucas swung around, his axe ready, only to see a frail woman at the fence. Showing no fear, she stood wrapped in her kangaroo skin and silently studied him. Her gaze was somehow different to those of other female visitors. To Lucas, it seemed to contain an element of knowing, as though she recognised him from somewhere, but if that was the case, she made no move toward him, nor did she speak.

Carrying nothing but a few wooden tools, it was obvious the woman had not come to trade. Her eyes searched his face then roamed over his body before pausing briefly on the whale's tooth hanging from his neck then again returning to rest on his face. She was curious, nothing more, he decided, and smiling, dropped the axe.

It was something in her smile, something warm and vaguely familiar. At first it came as a whisper, then as a deafening roar, crashing from one side of his brain to the other as the thought fought to the surface. The ground loomed upwards and began to spin. He grabbed the side of the hut to steady himself, trying to think above the pounding of his heart and the explosion in his head.

"Skylamahana," he whispered.

He wiped his sweating palms across the legs of his grubby trousers and started nervously toward her. He was a good head taller, and her hand brushed his cheek as she searched his eyes, smiling. Her gentle touch then trailed down his neck and, finding the cord, came to rest on the whale's tooth. A mist descended over the clear, dark-brown eyes that had moments before studied him so carefully. The smile faded, and without a word, she about-faced and darted toward the trees.

"Wait!" he cried. "Skylamahana! Mother . . . Mama . . . wait!"

The woman paid no heed, her steps light and nimble, and by the time Lucas reached the tall timbers, she had vanished. Although he knew there was little hope of finding her, a hunger from deep inside compelled him to search. Hours passed while he combed the undergrowth calling her name relentlessly, convinced she could hear him, but for some reason chose not to reveal herself. Only when the light faded did he admit defeat and turn toward the compound, his feet as heavy as his heart.

"I'm sure it was my mother," he later told Bess. "There was something in her eyes. We both recognised something. If only you'd been at the front of the hut instead of out the back washing, you would have seen her and been able to tell me for sure."

"It's been years since she brought the two of ya here," Bess sighed. "I's not so sure I'd know her now, anyways."

"She was looking at this." Lucas clutched the whale's tooth. "I'm sure she recognised it. It had to be her."

"Skylamahana it might a been, but it makes no difference now cause she's chosen not ta recognise ya as her son. Doing so could cause her even more grief, and ya don't want that, now do ya? Who knows what sort of situation she's in now . . . could get her cast out, even. It's better left forgotten."

But he could never forget.

The following year Lucas' curiosity led him to explore tribal society. He located a member of the Tommeginer band many miles southwest of the sealers camp and, through trade, was able to gain the man's trust enough to be allowed to accompany him back to the band's camp.

He received a cool, but polite, reception and with little understanding of their language and customs, he found it difficult to make himself understood. To his surprise, they knew who he was and where he lived on the coast. He learned his mother was of the Tommeginer band and, even though the old man was reluctant to talk, being the band's historian, he felt an obligation to the newcomer.

"Long ago, woman from here marry Pallitteeler warrior. Him killed in big fight. White man came with white baby . . . join Pallitteeler . . . took woman as wife. She had baby," the old man said, nodding to Lucas with full acknowledgement. "When white warrior left, woman go with Sulyukenny of the Tarkinener people to west coast. No more to tell."

"Did she have other children?" Lucas asked, taking another tack.

"Some before you . . . others after."

"Where are they now?"

"Them with Tarkinener mob."

Lucas was unable to find out more about Skylamahana because no one would speak her name, and because of this, he concluded his mother was now dead. He tried to ask why he and his brother were abandoned at the sealers' settlement, but the old historian merely shrugged. Either he didn't know the answer or he didn't understand the question. Perhaps he didn't *want* to understand the question.

Although he had several Tommeginer cousins remaining with the band, Lucas found no real acceptance, and he decided it was pointless to try to seek out his mother's other children. It would be no different with the Tarkinener. Here he was with his mother's people, a place where he should find solace, yet they were not his people, and he remained disillusioned and miserable.

Not one to give up easily, Lucas stayed on with the Tommeginer for several weeks, but was unable to build any significant relationships. In the end, he quietly slipped from the camp one morning, resolved to make the most of life as a sealer in a white man's world.

The resolution was short lived.

Chapter 42

"If you break it, you fix it, just like you did the door; ain't no two ways about it," Ezra Ford growled. "Then maybe next time, you'll think again before you go acting like a bull seal what's had its dinner snatched."

"He bloody had it coming," Lucas said.

"The furniture didn't," snapped Bess, busy gathering splintered wood from the corner of the cabin where the chair landed. "You has ta get used to people calling you a breed. They ain't gonna change. It's you that has ta change if you want peace in this life."

"I can't help the way I feel."

"You can feel as you will, but you'd best do something about your temper," Ezra said. "Anger like that will get you into more trouble the older you get. Best to harness it now before it gets out of hand. It's one thing to kick a hole in the door or smash a chair, but quite another to attack a man like you just did. Do that and you'll have the law after you."

"I didn't hit him hard."

"Makes no difference. He'll be out for revenge, especially as you strut about like a cockerel while he's limping off somewhere. Just because you're getting muscle on your bones, there's no reason to act like you just did. And you can't go round calling people 'one-eyed, white bastards' and expect to get away with it either."

"Well he shouldn't have called me a breed."

"But that's what you are, lad, a half-breed, just like Bessie and my kids are: white father and black mother. No sense getting riled up over the truth."

"But it's the word and the way they use it," Lucas lamented. "It's meant to be an insult."

"You'll always have trouble with folks that don't like what you are," Ezra said. "You have to ignore it and get on with life. It'll destroy you if you don't. That's what I've done. There's many a folk thinks I should have a white woman, but Bessie here suits me just fine, and who are they to say what's right for a man? I know the early sealers stole women from the North-West tribe, bedded them then used them as slaves. I'm not one of them. True, Bess was taken from the Pennemukeer band before she came into my hands, but she's happy now. Is that not right, Bessie?"

Although she nodded, Lucas long ago recognised deep sadness in her eyes. On questioning, Bess had simply shrugged and talked about changing times, but it was clear she still mourned her people and a previous way of life.

"Best ta get on with the life ya got than fretting over the life ya ain't got no more," she quipped.

"That's right," Ezra said. "It mightn't be a grand life, but we're happy. There's a roof over our heads and food on the table in return for honest work . . . well, mostly, anyway. A man can't ask for much more."

"Do you ever wish you were back with your tribe?" Lucas asked.

"I don't think about it now," Bess replied. "My children are here, so it's where I be staying."

"It would be different if it wasn't for the whites."

"What are you saying, lad?" Ezra's eyes flashed a warning.

"The tribes were happy until the Europeans came and spoiled things. They're to blame. Not you of course," Lucas glanced warily at Ezra. "You're different. It's the ones who think they've a right to do just as they please, and to hell with anyone else. They're the ones who think they're so high and mighty, and they're the ones who call me breed. I hate them . . . all of them."

Lucas thought he caught a spark of understanding in Bess' eyes, but it vanished in an instant. "I used ta feel like that, but hating ain't the answer," she said. "Ya has ta find what's inside of you. That's what gives ya strength."

"That's easy for you to say, but I don't want anything more to do with whites," Lucas glowered. "They're two-faced, and I'm done with them, as well as my father's name. I'm not going to keep it any longer. Lucas Thomas is dead. From now on, I'll be calling myself Luke Skye."

In denying his father's name, Lucas sought to deny the pain associated with his mixed blood. He knew the whites would never see beyond his colour. In choosing the shortened version of his mother's name, he told himself he would be more aboriginal than white, maybe making him stronger and less susceptible to white man's taunting. But although Lucas paid outward allegiance to his native heritage, both Ezra and Bess knew he still harboured resentment for the colour of his skin.

"My advice to you, lad, is do what's in your heart," Ezra

said. "If your conscience is clear, then you've got nothing to answer for. Sure you can get angry and it's all too easy to smash furniture and belt people up when you do, but when you're done with it, will you honestly be able to say it was right? Where is your dignity . . . and pride? That's what my father used to ask. You've got to ask yourself the question, and you need to know the answer before you start in on someone . . . because it's too late afterwards."

Lucas clenched his jaw. He heard the words. They were easy to say. And they did not alter the fact that his dark skin had branded him something less than a white man in the eyes of Europeans. He would keep his pride, he decided, but he would also keep his rage.

The first talk of change came when Luke was around fourteen years of age.

"It's time to move from here," Ezra said. "Sealing's pretty well dried up in these parts."

"From what I hear, it's much the same all along the north coast," Evan Mortimer replied. "There's only the south or the big islands left."

Lucas, repositioning a log with the poker, strained to listen above the crackle from the fireplace.

"The south's too cold," Ezra commented.

"And too bloody rugged. I reckon the eastern islands, the Furneaux group, would be the best move."

"What about King's Island?"

"Ain't the coast rugged there as well?"

"Aye, that it is," Ezra confirmed. "But the sealing's still good, and I hear there's next to no one living on it. Cain't say the same for the Furneaux Islands. Lots of sealers there I hear. Most of them are associated with the Bass Strait companies. It'll soon dry up."

"I vote for King's Island if it's unsettled," shot in Luke. "It'd be like having our own island."

"We all know what you want," laughed Ezra. "You'd be a hermit if given half the chance."

"Well, if you decide on King's Island, you can count me out," Evan said. "I prefer the climate of the eastern islands and the security of maybe working for one of the companies. I reckon a few of the others will feel the same way."

It was only a matter of weeks before the sealers began to break camp. Most of the group intended to settle in the Furneaux Islands, but Ezra and Luke chose the more craggy King's Island, which lay off the northwest tip of Van Diemen's Land. It had been Ezra's choice not only because of the excellent sealing opportunities, but because its remoteness offered Luke and his own children refuge from an unaccepting world.

It never occurred to him that Bess, let alone their children, would not want to accompany him, but Bess was adamant.

"I was born on this here land and I's not about to leave it. Men took me away once, and it was just luck that I's brought back and a good man got me, but as good as ya are, Ezra, I ain't about to follow ya to no island. My spirit belongs in the land of my people and I's staying right here."

"I can't leave Mama here alone," Caleb, their eldest son, said. "I'll be staying here with her."

"Me too," chorused the others.

Ezra paled. "So be it," he said slowly, quietly, from within a newfound contemplation. "I'll not force any of you to go against your will or conscience. Luke and I will go alone."

But when the time came to leave his family Ezra changed his mind. "You go on, lad. I can't leave them here alone. You know that," he said. "There'll be a good living for you on King's Island, and there'll be no one to rile you like here. Maybe that temper will cool off a bit. Go with my blessing . . . and God be with you."

Despite the sudden pang in his chest, Luke put his face to the wind and stepped forward, for looking back only held misery, and he had no time for tears.

A new life waited.

By the end of the week, Luke found himself on a lonely beach near the northwest tip of Van Diemen's Land, wondering how he was going to get to King's Island. He was exhausted, cold, and hungry. Staring down at the pile of sticks and kindling in front of him, he cursed the wretched wind that prevented him from lighting them. He'd killed a small wallaby and wanted to eat, but he didn't want it raw—needed a hot meal, one that would chase the chill from his bones.

A strong gust of wind scattered his sticks, and he scrambled to retrieve them. It was pointless staying on the beach. The shelter he needed could only be found inland. He hauled his rucksack onto his back, gathered his weapons and other belongings from the sand, and walked toward the trees.

The fire was easily started once he found a sheltered spot, and within minutes, he'd fashioned a spit and had a meaty wallaby thigh roasting over it. All he had to do now was wait while it cooked. He watched the flames for a while until the beach beckoned—as it always did.

Luke's thoughts turned to his brother as he settled himself on a sand dune overlooking the coastline and stared across the ocean in the direction of where he supposed his brother might be. Could Buck be in a similar plight? Did he have enough to eat? Was he warm? Was he happy? Could he get along with the people he, himself, found intolerable? He set his jaw against the sudden misting of his eyes as a low groan broke from his lungs, and he fell backward onto the sand.

One day he would know.

Epilogue

Emmeline Thornridge gave birth to a golden-haired daughter not long after Nicholas Thomas left Sydney Town. Her disappointed husband accepted the child as his own rather than face the humiliation of it becoming public knowledge that he'd been cuckolded, which would certainly happen if he turned his wife and the baby out. With time he grew to love the child, thought of her as his daughter in every way, and she wanted for nothing.

Lieutenant John Bowen left the Derwent in August 1804 and by January 1805 was on his way to England. In May of that year he was promoted to commander, became captain in 1806, and for the next three years, he took part in the British blockade of Martinique and Guadeloupe in the Caribbean.

In February 1811 he wrote to the undersecretary of state for the colonies, requesting he succeed Collins as lieutenant governor of Van Diemen's Land, but it was suggested that as a naval officer he could not command troops. Bowen wrote again disagreeing with the decision and emphasised his long and sincere interest in the colony since his days at Risdon, but he was denied the position. He wrote again the following year requesting he be considered if it became vacant again.

It was never to be.

Instead, Bowen continued on with a distinguished, if short, naval career which included captaining several ships and meeting Napoleon Bonaparte on St. Helena. Upon returning to England in 1825, he married Elizabeth Lindley Clowes and died in 1827 at the age of forty-seven.

Martha Hayes chose to remain in Van Diemen's Land with her parents after Bowen's departure. She gave birth to his second daughter, Martha Charlotte, some months later. Prior to his leaving, Bowen had organised for Martha to assume the status of "settler" so she would qualify for a land grant, and in 1811 she married her neighbour, Andrew Whitehead, who had been a convict with Collins' party.

Although Bowen never met his second daughter, he maintained contact and sent her silverware when she married in 1823. His older daughter, Henrietta, had died earlier that same year.

Nicholas Thomas didn't make the trek back to the Derwent; instead he surrendered himself to the authorities at Port Dalrymple and was subsequently transferred to Hobart. From there he was transported to Sydney for court marshal. He was found guilty of desertion, the penalty for which was execution by firing squad.

Nicholas' sons, Buck and Lucas, brothers and best friends in childhood, assumed separate and very different lives following their separation. Buck's new life with the McCabe family was one of privilege, education, and commerce. Lucas, on the other hand, faced discrimination, poverty, and hardship.

Neither brother could forget the other, and separation was a heavy burden, as was the loss of their happy, carefree childhood, but neither gave up hope they would one day be reunited.

Their descendants were born into the life each man created for himself, within the confines of colonial-society attitudes in a penal settlement, and the differences between the two were striking and often heartbreaking.

You have finished reading

The Soldier's Seed

Book One
of
Southern Skyes

Please continue on to a sneak preview of:

The Divergence

Book Two
of
Southern Skyes

The Divergence

Chapter 1

Thomas Buck McCabe was baptised in the little church at Norfolk Plains within weeks of the family taking him in. From the beginning, the boy was headstrong, refusing to answer to anything other than "Buck," but this wilful side to his nature demonstrated strength of character, and an indulgent James McCabe was secretly proud. And yet he could not, and would not, accept that Buck had an aboriginal brother somewhere on the coast, no matter how much the boy insisted.

"But I do so have a brother." Buck's new boots raised puffs of dirt as he stamped in frustration. "His name is Lucas, and he lives with the sealers."

"The child would have no reason to fabricate," Ann commented.

But James didn't want to believe or understand, refusing to deal with the possibility of his precious new son having a black relative. The notion was downright loathsome.

"Why a man would want to cohabit with a black woman and produce half-breeds is beyond me. The races were never meant to mix, of that I'm sure. They're different in every way."

"It's only natural when there aren't enough women in the colony," Anne said.

"Well, to my mind, a little abstinence wouldn't go astray. Where's their self-respect?"

Ann looked away, not answering, for she knew the ways of men.

Buck continued to talk of his brother for months after his adoption, but Big Buck Jones had long since departed with his ship, so there was no one to confirm his story. Since he could not read, Buck had no knowledge of the evidence borne by his fob watch—the names his father had years ago scratched into the timepiece he now showed James.

"This is an expensive item," James said, rolling the gold watch over in his palm, its chain swinging freely. "Where did you get it?"

"It belonged to my real father," Buck said proudly.

"Could it be stolen?"

"Oh no, sir," Buck said, shocked by the suggestion. "It's mine. I've always had it. Open it. There's writing inside."

James released the clasp and felt the blood drain from his face as he read the names *Lucas William Thomas, Nicholas Thomas, Margaret McKinnon, Buck William Thomas (1804) and Lucas (1805)*. It was the last name that hit like the kick of a cannon. So the boy was right. He did have a brother.

Only the first name looked professionally engraved. The others were crudely scratched into the metal so he concluded the original owner would have been Lucas William Thomas, who perhaps gave the watch to his son, Nicholas. For a moment James entertained the possibility that Buck had scratched in the names, but the boy could not yet read and write.

The numbers following the last two names could only refer

to the year of birth, and their mother would seem to be a woman named Margaret McKinnon, certainly not an aboriginal name. But why did the surname not follow the name of Lucas? James looked at his son and sighed. The evidence spoke for itself. He could no longer argue.

Buck cut into James' thoughts. "What does it say?"

"It mentions someone called Lucas who is a year younger than you," he said quietly, reluctantly. There was no sense in avoiding the truth. Buck would soon enough be able to read the names for himself.

"My brother," Buck said, his face radiant. "So now you know I wasn't making up a story. You can believe me."

"Yes, I believe you."

"Will you go and get him now?"

James frowned. If he could be certain Lucas was white, he would be delighted to have another son, but he couldn't be sure, and a dark-skinned boy was entirely out of the question. While ever there was doubt, he was not about to take the risk.

"That won't be possible, Buck. Besides, we don't know where he is."

"But we could search the north coast. That's where he lives . . . at the sealers' camp."

"That's a lot of coastline. The likelihood of us ever locating a child is too slim. No, we'd be wasting our time."

"But we could try, couldn't we, Papa? Please."

"No. There is more important work to be done here, and we won't be able to find him, you know that." James stood in an effort to end the conversation and moved towards the door.

"No I don't," Buck said through pouting lips. "If we looked hard enough, we could find him."

"What's done is done," James said, steeling himself. "Lucas

belongs in the past, and I'll hear no more of it. Those times are over." He left the room, leaving Buck to stare at his feet, but he returned minutes later carrying a small wooden box. He seated himself on the maroon couch next to Buck, whose eyes still glistened with fought-back tears, and placed his arm across the boy's sagging shoulders.

"I'm not a heartless man, Buck," James said quietly. "And I understand you loved your brother, but you must accept that you have a new life now, a better life, and as my son you'll want for nothing. Be happy with what you have. I doubt that we could ever find Lucas, but I shall make some inquiries to see if he can be located."

"Oh, thank you, Papa." Buck flung his arms around his father's neck, knocking the wooden box to the floor.

"Now don't get your hopes up too high," James said, breaking free and retrieving the box from the thick, red mat covering the centre of the room. "I'm not promising anything. Like I said, finding the camp will be difficult and a search would likely turn up nothing, but I will try. In the meantime, I want you to concentrate on your studies. A man is nothing without knowing how to read and write."

"And ride a horse," Buck said, pleased he could now stay in the saddle for a slow canter.

"That too," James smiled, pleased by the boy's changed disposition. "Look here," he said, placing the wooden box on his lap. "I want you to have this for your fob watch. It will keep it safe. Such a fine timepiece needs to be preserved. I used it for cufflinks, but it's yours now for the watch."

Buck undid the tiny clip and lifted the hinged lid of the intricately carved box to reveal its black velvet lining. It was indeed a box befitting a fine watch.

From then on Buck began to adapt quickly to his new home, excelling at all outdoor activities, especially the riding lessons given by James. Outwardly he appeared happy and content, the perfect son, but at his core burned a deep homesickness unseen by others, and he continued to pine for his brother. "Have they found Lucas yet?" It was the question he asked relentlessly.

"No news yet, son," was James' standard reply.

Ultimately the boy grew weary of hearing the same disinterested answer and eventually stopped asking, just as James had planned. The fact that his new father had no intention of keeping his word, and hadn't made inquiries, never once enter Buck's mind. He was far too trusting.

James, satisfied with his tactic, came to believe his son had finally moved on from his old life and considered the subject closed, but Buck's restraint in verbalising his thoughts did not mean he had forgotten. Nor was it indicative of diminished yearning. Buck new he would never erase Lucas from his mind and vowed that one day he would find him—and with no one else's help, if it came to that.

There were times when he so desperately wanted to return to the familiarity of the sealers' camp that he sought comfort in being alone in the bush. He would spend hours by himself just wandering and thinking. Only then could he recapture anything close to his past life of freedom and independence, but it was ultimately the company he craved, someone his own age to share the games and adventure. It was at these times tears welled in his eyes. Visions of his brother running along the beach, screaming, pleading, "Bucky, wait for me," brought forth emotions too powerful to stifle, but being too proud to show any sign of weakness, he succumbed only when he was alone.

"Cry baby bunting, Daddy's gone a hunting," chanted Rebecca, coming upon her new brother's hiding place between the bean vines behind the wood shed.

"Go away," he whimpered, cross at being discovered, and he quickly smeared tears across his dusty cheeks with a fist. After a severe scolding, the result of his long absences and wayward activities in the bush, Buck had agreed to his parents' demand that he remain close to home for a while and, in so doing, had been force to find a new refuge. Not counting on the inquisitive nature of his stickybeak sister, he thought the bean patch would be free from prying eyes.

"What's the matter?"

"Nothing."

"Boys aren't supposed to cry."

Buck ignored her, staring at the ground from his squatting position amid the green vines.

"Well?" she probed. "Must be something wrong."

"None of your business," he mumbled.

"You're a sook."

"Get lost."

"You're rude too. I'm going to tell." She whirled around in a flounce of powder-blue linen and skipped towards the house renewing her "cry baby" chant.

His new big sister, Buck decided, was a stupid little tattletale, and from then on, he reserved his tears for the solitude of his bed.

Sharyn's Story

Sharyn Bradford Lunn was born in Sydney, Australia, though she is accustomed to both "the big smoke" and rural hideaways as her family shifted from her birthplace to a small country town and back again during her childhood. She briefly worked in a telephone exchange then a kindergarten before embarking on a career in nursing.

After reading Alex Haley's *Roots*, she developed a passion for genealogy and history that deepened with the ensuing years. This went hand in hand with another newly discovered interest: writing. And so a series was born.

When not writing or researching, Sharyn can be found enjoying time at home on the Central Coast with family and friends, swimming, walking her dogs, reading, tracing someone's family tree, or enjoying a rock concert. She digs a good rollercoaster ride as much as a trail bike ride. To round out her adventurer's spirit, she embraces a joy of travel and learning about other cultures.

Look for more from Sharyn in the coming months and years, as she develops her *Southern Skyes* series and tinkers in other writing endeavours.

Message From the Author

One last thing . . .

As you close the last pages of this book, you will have opportunities to rate *The Soldier's Seed*, make comments, and share your thoughts on places like Goodreads, Facebook, and Twitter. If you believe the book is worth sharing, would you take a few seconds to let your friends know about it?

If it brings enjoyment to their lives, they'll be grateful to you. As I will.

All the best,

Sharyn Bradford Lunn

For more information about the books in the series, including sneak peeks and more, go to www.sharynbradfordlunnauthor.com.